OP. 6⁵ᶜ

All
Wild
Creatures
Welcome

Also by Patricia Curtis

The Animal Shelter
Animal Partners
Greff: The Story of a Guide Dog
Cindy, A Hearing Ear Dog
The Indoor Cat
Animal Rights

Lifeline for Wildlife student intern Jamie Morales checks the wing action of a young blue jay before releasing it.

All Wild Creatures Welcome

The Story of a Wildlife Rehabilitation Center

Patricia Curtis

photographs by David Cupp

LODESTAR BOOKS · E. P. Dutton · New York

Library of Congress Cataloging in Publication Data

Curtis, Patricia, date.
   All wild creatures welcome.

   "Lodestar books."
   Includes index.
   Summary: Describes the work of the wildlife
rehabilitation center in Stony Point, New York, how
it came to be established and how it handles the many
wild animals that are brought to it for treatment.
Includes a list of similar rehabilitation centers
throughout the country arranged by region.
   1. Wildlife rescue—New York (State)—Stony Point—
Juvenile literature.   2. Lifeline for Wildlife
(Veterinary hospital)—Juvenile literature.
[1. Wildlife rescue—New York (State)—Stony Point.
2. Lifeline for Wildlife (Veterinary hospital)]
I. Cupp, David, ill.   II. Title.
QL83.2.C87   1985   636.089   84-28756
ISBN 0-525-67164-1

Published in the United States by E. P. Dutton,
2 Park Avenue, New York, N.Y. 10016

Published simultaneously in Canada by
Fitzhenry & Whiteside Limited, Toronto

Editor: Virginia Buckley   Designer: Isabel Warren-Lynch

Printed in the U.S.A.   COBE   First Edition
10 9 8 7 6 5 4 3 2 1

*to Hope Sawyer Buyukmihci,
who provides refuge and protection
for all wild creatures*

Acknowledgments

I wish to express first of all my deepest thanks to Betsy Lewis, Mark Lerman, and the staff of Lifeline for Wildlife, without whose full cooperation David Cupp and I could not have created this book. It was an exciting experience for me to learn so much about wild animals and birds from the compassionate and knowledgeable people at Lifeline.

I am also grateful to others who helped me with information and advice: my friend Hope Ryden, the naturalist / writer / photographer; Susan Hagood of Defenders of Wildlife; Guy Hodge of the Humane Society of the United States; and Kathleen Savesky of the National Association for the Advancement of Humane Education. My thanks also to rehabilitators Maxine Guy; Curtiss Clumpner of HOWL (Help Our Wildlife); Ralph T. Heath, Jr., of the Suncoast Seabird Sanctuary; Richard and Adele Evans of the National Wildlife Rehabilitators Association; and the board of the Wildlife Rehabilitation Council.

Patricia Curtis

Contents

1 • The Wildlife Hospital • 1
2 • Lifeline Beginnings • 17
3 • The Veterinarian • 31
4 • Rescues • 42
5 • Caring People • 54
6 • Valuable Lives • 64
7 • Interns Speak • 79
8 • Other Rehabilitators • 93
9 • What You Can Do To Help Wildlife • 105
   Additional Information • 116
   Wildlife Rehabilitators • 119
   Index • 123

Those who wish to pet and baby wild animals, "love" them. But those who respect their natures and wish to let them live normal lives, love them more.

Edwin Way Teale
Circle of the Seasons

1 The Wildlife Hospital

It is a spring afternoon in a wooded suburban community in New York State, and the veterinary hospital of Lifeline for Wildlife is filled with patients. Most are furred or feathered patients, in cages stacked about the large room. Some, however, are so young they have neither fur nor feathers but just naked skin, their eyes and ears still tightly closed. They are lying under heat lamps or are snuggled in soft rags in boxes set on heating pads.

Twelve active and chattering juvenile gray squirrels are chasing one another around on some thick branches that have been secured upright in their tall cage. Some of them are there because they fell out of nests that were destroyed; some were orphaned; all would have died from exposure or starvation or been killed by other animals if they had not been found by compassionate people who brought them to Lifeline.

A big raccoon glowers from his cage and makes it clear to everyone that he wants his freedom. He was a pet until his owners grew tired of him, especially since he was no longer the cute, cuddly baby they had found in the woods last summer. He became a restless, destructive, and often irritable adult. Sometimes he snapped at people. The owners realized their mistake in keeping him in the first place and turned him over to Lifeline. The job of rehabilitating him to survive in the wild has begun.

A sparrow huddles forlornly in the corner of its box. Trapped accidentally in a man's garage, it panicked and flew into a can of oil. The man called Lifeline, and a staff member went and captured the oil-soaked little creature. Now, it has been cleaned, is beginning to eat, and probably will live.

A muskrat with a bad wound healing on her back, apparently hit by a car, is solemnly eating spinach leaves. Two young skunks are gobbling up a mash of dog food mixed with milk formula and getting it all over their glossy black-and-white faces. A crow with a bandaged foot hobbles about in a cage next to that of a big turtle with a bandaged shell. Nestled quietly in a large cage in a corner is a spotted buck fawn who apparently was attacked, perhaps by dogs. The veterinarian sewed up his wounds, and everyone is trying to help him pull through. And everywhere, everywhere, dozens of baby birds peep and chirp in makeshift nests.

In all, some seventy-five infant, sick, or injured wild creatures are being cared for in this room.

Two young women, Shari Stahl and Valerie Plesko, are busily cleaning cages. They remove each animal temporarily, handling it carefully so as not to frighten it or get hurt themselves. Then they scrub the cage with disinfectant, lay down clean newspapers, fill the drinking bowl with fresh water, and return the animal, putting food in after it.

"The animals stay nice and clean for about two minutes," says dark-eyed Shari. "Then they tip over their water bowls, throw their food around, urinate and defecate all over the place, and turn themselves and their cages into wet, gooey chaos again. Wild animals are clean in their natural habitats, but in cages they can't help getting themselves filthy."

"This is no place for anybody who can't stand mess or who gets disgusted easily," adds sixteen-year-old Valerie cheerfully.

But the girls know that the work they are doing is crucial to the survival of these seventy-five wild animals and birds.

Moving among the cages is a small, green-eyed woman who looks not much older than Shari and Valerie and is also dressed in blue jeans, a T-shirt, and sneakers, her long straight brown hair piled casually on her head. She is, however, very much in charge. This entire scene in the veterinary hospital has come about through her inspiration, leadership, and hard, dedicated work.

She is Betsy Lewis, founder and executive director of Lifeline for Wildlife.

She stops by a cage of baby opossums who have managed to create just the kind of mess Shari described. "I think you'd better bathe them one by one under warm running water, towel them off, and then put them in a box on a heating pad to finish drying while you clean their cage," she says to Shari.

When Betsy looks at the crowd of vigorous young squirrels who are scampering about in their cage, she notices that a little one is crouched by itself. She picks it up. "I think you're too puny

An infant raccoon, so young its eyes aren't yet open, is examined by Lifeline for Wildlife's director.

to be in with those roughnecks," she says to the tiny animal. She kisses it and gently sets it in a small cage with an infant squirrel who has no hair yet and is sleeping under a heat lamp for warmth.

As she passes the adult raccoon who had been a pet, she bangs sharply on his cage a few times. The animal shrinks back and hisses. "We have to teach you to be afraid of people if you're going to survive in the wild," says Betsy. "Right now, you're too tame."

"Ah—you ate some of your fish, that's good," she remarks to a green heron, who looks rather glum. "I've been worried about this bird," she explains. "She was brought in with a broken wing —from a gunshot, Mark thinks." Dr. Mark Lerman is Lifeline's veterinarian. "He bandaged it, but he wants to wait until she begins to eat and is less stressed before he anesthetizes her, cleans out the wound, and sets the bones."

Three young opossums are quarreling in their cage. Betsy reaches into the big refrigerator that stands against the wall, removes the body of a baby rabbit that died of an injury the day before and, without batting an eye, takes a knife and slits it down the middle, pulling open the flesh. Then she gives the carcass to the opossums, who stop fighting immediately and fall upon it, tearing into it with their little sharp white teeth, their bright eyes shining. Opossums are omnivores—that is, they'll eat just about everything, including meat, fruit, vegetables, eggs, insects, and reptiles.

Opossums are not pretty animals, nor are they very bright, but at Lifeline they receive the same devoted care as all the other animals. In terms of the value placed on their lives, creatures such as skunks and opossums are the equals of cute raccoons and beautiful fawns. The Lifeline staff carefully lives up to the organization's credo: Every Life Unique; All Life Sacred.

Opossums are very primitive animals—their ancestors coexisted with dinosaurs—and in the history of life-forms on earth, they are considered great survivors. They're our only native American marsupials (animals such as kangaroos, whose young are carried in a pouch on the female's belly). Infant opossums are

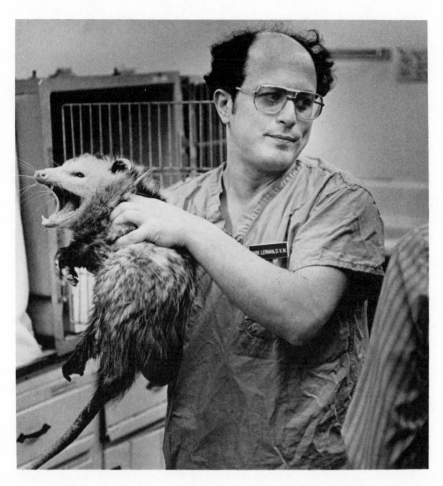

The veterinarian with a protesting patient—an opossum

scarcely more than embryos when they're born, yet they must crawl, naked and blind, up the mother's body and into her pouch without any help. Even though the mother has only thirteen nipples, about twenty infants are born at a time. That's nature's way of ensuring that at least some will make the journey successfully. Among most wild animals, many more are born than live to grow up.

The stronger and luckier infant opossums who make it to the mother's pouch attach themselves to nipples and stay there for about two months. Lifeline recommends that anyone who finds a dead female opossum look in her pouch. If there are babies still attached to the nipples, the mother's body should be brought to the hospital without disturbing the infants. That will give them a better chance for survival.

Shari, putting the nine baby opossums back in their clean cage, notices that one seems weak and unusually quiet. Trained by Betsy to pay attention to even slight symptoms among the patients, Shari knows something is wrong, so she removes this little one to a box by itself.

"You're right—it is sick," says Betsy when Shari calls her attention to the infant. She takes it to Mark, who examines it and shakes his head.

"I don't know what's the matter with it," he says. "Just give it supportive care."

"Opossums used to be native only in the southern states, but as their habitat there has shrunk, they have gradually moved north," Betsy continues on the subject of opossums. "Those that are brought to us in winter are often suffering from frostbite of the ears and toes—they're not well adapted to cold weather. Yet they're amazingly hardy. We rarely lose full-grown opossums."

There may be an exception today. Betsy opens a cage where a thin, middle-aged female opossum is sleeping under a blanket. "She was found lying on a lawn, unable to move," Betsy remarks. "The finder took her to the American Society for the Prevention of Cruelty to Animals (ASPCA) in New York City, who in turn called us to come and get her." She touches the animal's paper-thin ear and adjusts the blanket. "She is too sick to eat, but she'd die if she became dehydrated, so Mark is giving her supportive fluids intravenously as well as regular doses of antibiotics. We haven't been able to find out what's wrong with her. Many wild animals come in half-dead and recover after receiving just supportive care, while others don't make it no matter what we do for them.

"In her case, Mark thinks she has a chance. But if she dies, and we get other sick opossums in the meantime, we may send her body to the laboratory for an autopsy or to Richard Evans, a veterinary pathologist we know in Illinois who is also a wildlife rehabilitator. We'll want to know what she had, so perhaps we can save similar cases in the future."

Now Betsy turns to the fawn. "Valerie, will you help me tube-feed him?" she asks, preparing a bucket of milk formula. The fawn has persistently refused to nurse from a bottle, so it is necessary to give him nourishment through a tube to his stomach. Betsy kneels on the floor with the young animal between her knees and quickly, expertly, passes a soft rubber tube down his throat. Valerie holds the bucket and, with a large syringe, pumps the formula into the tube.

If Betsy were less experienced, less careful, she might not have gotten the tube down the fawn's esophagus into his stomach, but down his windpipe instead, thereby filling his lungs with milk and drowning him. "I accidentally killed an animal that way before I learned how to do this right," she admits.

When she is satisfied that the fawn has had enough, Lifeline's director proceeds to feed the other creatures that are too young to eat normally. When infant animals are with their mothers, they instinctively know how to nurse. But when they're orphaned very young and put in an artificial environment, they won't instinctively suck at the nipple of a nursing bottle right away and must be fed through a tube or medicine dropper.

Several six-day-old baby squirrels, a late litter, must be tube-fed every four hours; this means that they will go home with Betsy at the end of the day, and she will set the alarm clock and get up to feed them during the night, every night, as long as they need it.

She picks up one of the squirrels and deftly slips a tube that looks hardly thicker than a hair down its throat. In a minute or two, she examines its stomach.

"You can see when its stomach is full—look," she says. Through the thin skin, the milk can be made out, and it appears that the tiny stomach is indeed full. She holds the odd-looking infant, still blind and hairless, to her lips for a second before tenderly returning it to its box—a gesture she repeats often with the very young animals and birds.

Betsy holds a quick conference with Judy, who is preparing a feeding tube.

Betsy tube-feeds an infant pigeon.

This baby squirrel must be given nourishment through a tube to its stomach. Below: The tube in place, Judy uses a syringe to push the milk formula slowly into the squirrel's stomach.

A two-week-old raccoon, its eyes still closed, is squeaking in a box. Betsy opens the box. Holding the tiny wildling on its back, she addresses it maternally. "Let's see if we have diarrhea again. If so, we're not going to eat right now." She massages the raccoon's stomach to stimulate defecation. All is well, so Betsy gives the animal some milk from a baby bottle. When she rubs the back of its neck, it makes the typical raccoon sound of pleasure—a chortle rather like a cat's purr.

The next creature that requires Betsy's help is a big gray-and-white herring gull. He is so depressed in captivity that he refuses to eat, and the Lifeline staff is hard pressed to keep him alive so that his bumblefoot, an infection common among birds, can be treated. Betsy lifts the gull from his cage and sits down on the floor with him.

"I wish you'd start to eat on your own," she says to the big bird, wrestling to get a good grip on him and opening his bill. Quickly she drops some small fish called smelts into the reluctant bird's bill. He swallows. She feeds him this way until she thinks he's had enough, then puts him back in his cage.

"Try to stay away from this side of the room and speak softly so as not to disturb him," Betsy advises Shari and Valerie. "He'll vomit if he gets upset, and we want him to keep his food down."

Shari and Valerie, having cleaned all the cages for the moment, are now feeding baby birds, who gape—open their beaks wide —and cry whenever anyone passes by. They must be fed every twenty minutes, from morning to night. The girls use medicine droppers to put food down the eager little throats.

"Sometimes it seems never ending—putting food in one end, and cleaning up the other," Shari declares with a little sigh.

When the baby birds are older, they will be put with adolescent birds who know how to peck food and drink water; the little ones will learn from them by imitating.

Judy Lapine, Betsy's right-hand staff member, puts her head in the door. "A woman is here with a pigeon she found wandering in the middle of a road," Judy reports. "It's a racing pigeon and it's malnourished, but I don't believe it's hurt. Could you come and look at it, Betsy?"

A gaping baby bird in a paper-cup nest is fed with a medicine dropper.

A woman is holding a white pigeon on a table in an examining room. "I think it must have been hit by a car, because it doesn't seem to be able to fly, it only staggers," she tells Betsy.

Betsy examines the bird and perches it on her finger. "It's not injured," she tells the woman. "This is a racing pigeon—you can see the band on its leg. It's simply starved and exhausted." She thanks the woman for bringing in the bird and puts it in a cage with two other pigeons. The racing pigeon very soon begins to eat.

"Racing pigeons are often raced until they burn up all their energy and collapse," Betsy explains. "People find them and bring them to us. We try to identify the birds' owners and notify them, but usually they aren't interested—they almost never take the trouble to come and get their birds. We keep racing pigeons until they gain normal weight and strength, and then we release them in areas where there are other pigeons around. If they want to go home, they can."

The lively young squirrels in the cage with the branches will almost certainly all reach adulthood and be released in the woods. The sparrow will soon be able to fly again and will simply be set free.

The raccoon who had been a pet will be moved to Lifeline's other facility in Ellenville, New York, and introduced to a peer group of raccoons about his age in a large outdoor enclosure. The other raccoons will huff and stamp at him for perhaps twenty-four hours and then will accept him. From them, he will learn much of what being a raccoon is about. If a pet that's normally a wild animal is not handled but is kept for a while with others of its own kind who are wild, eventually it will revert to wildness. After two or three months in the outdoor cage, the raccoons will be taken to a deeply wooded area, away from human habitation, and given their freedom together.

At the time the scenes in this book take place, Lifeline for Wildlife operates in two facilities. The veterinary hospital and office are located in the suburban village of Monsey, New York, while the country property, with the farmhouse and outdoor cages, is seventy miles away in Ellenville. Dr. Mark Lerman and Betsy are usually at the veterinary hospital and office, but the rest of the staff works in either place, wherever they're most needed.

All the animals and birds that survive at the hospital but need

In the outdoor enclosure at the Ellenville Center, above, a young raccoon peeks out of its shelter, and below, four little raccoons explore a hollow log.

Young raccoons are about to learn what a fish looks, smells, and tastes like in the wild. Yum-yum.

time to become strong and healthy are transferred to the Ellen-ville facility. There they live in large outdoor cages, usually with others of their kind, until they are completely grown, healed, or recovered. When they are ready, they are taken to suitable wil-derness areas and released.

In the years since she founded Lifeline for Wildlife, Betsy Lewis· has seen many thousands of wildlings brought in sick, injured, or orphaned, sometimes half-dead, sometimes so young they look like little more than fetuses. She and her colleagues try to cope with the results of every kind of human cruelty or natural hazard encountered by animals and birds in the wild. It's painful when their patients die, but more than half live to be released in their natural habitats.

There are many caring people engaged in wildlife rehabilitation work throughout the United States, and they return to the wild those creatures that can make it. They are careful not to make pets of the wildlings and try to preserve as much as possible the creatures' instinctual fear of human beings. This fear is essential to their survival.

Obviously, the rewards in this work are not the same as the satisfaction of restoring sick or injured pets to health. Rehabili-tated wildlings will not give years of loving companionship, as pets will. They will run or fly away as fast as they can, maybe after literally biting the hand that has fed them. They hurry back to their normal habits and habitats without so much as a backward glance at the people who saved them.

It takes a special kind of person to work hard to save an animal's life, to help it become healthy and independent, and then to set it free and never see it again. Yet the people at Lifeline for Wildlife find their work not only worthwhile but spiritually fulfilling.

In spite of supportive care, the tiny sick opossum dies dur-ing the night. Everyone is saddened momentarily, for every life is unique. But the hospital is pulsing with the living, all of whom need attention, so the work goes on without missing a beat.

2 Lifeline Beginnings

"My first experience with a wild animal came about when I was a teenager living at my mother's house in the country," Betsy relates. She is sitting at her cluttered desk in Lifeline's office, opening mail. Judy Lapine is on the telephone at her desk nearby, helping someone who has called for advice about a wild animal. Shari Stahl is sitting on the floor, stuffing the latest issue of the Lifeline newsletter into envelopes addressed to the membership. The only creature not busy is one of Betsy's dogs who, unconcerned, is asleep in a chair. Betsy is talking about the origins of Lifeline for Wildlife.

"I found a female baby woodchuck, out of the burrow, helpless, with no mother anywhere around," she continues. "I checked back later, several times, and she was still there, alone, acting distressed. I knew I had to do something. There was no such thing as a wildlife rehabilitation center where I could take her, so I brought her home and bottle-fed her with animal milk-replacement formula. She not only lived but thrived! I named her Mouska. Caring for that animal and watching her grow was a revelation to me—I was simply enthralled with nurturing her.

"Nevertheless, after several months, when she was grown, I released her in a field. I felt a terrible loss, but I knew it was the right thing to do. Even though she had been a pet, I counted on her instincts to be in working order once she reached sexual maturity. She showed up at the house a few times and lived on my mother's property for a while, then finally disappeared."

This experience had an influence on the work Betsy ultimately chose and the organization she created. But that didn't happen overnight.

Betsy Lewis graduated from a Midwestern college and decided to go into the antiques business. She and a classmate formed a partnership and became successful. "We had a funny shop where my three mongrel dogs were always sleeping on the antique sofas," she recalls with a smile. "It was a valuable year— I learned how to run a business."

But Betsy had an ambition that many young people share—a desire to help animals in some direct way. So she began traveling into New York City every day to work at the ASPCA, helping out in the adoptions department. After a few months, she moved to a job at an animal shelter in the country near her home. "There I was a kennel helper—cleaned out cages, fed the animals, that sort of thing," she says.

"One day, a construction worker brought in a baby starling that had fallen out of its nest on the construction site. The nest had been destroyed, so he couldn't put the starling back. This big burly man cared enough about that tiny bird's survival to bring it to the animal shelter. The shelter people had no experience with or interest in wildlife, so I brought the bird home and took care of it the best I could. I named it Hardhat, after the construction worker. I didn't know much, then, about baby birds, but I must have done the right thing, because Hardhat lived. I set him free when he was old enough to fly well.

"Soon after that, a woman brought in six orphaned baby rabbits. The shelter manager was about to euthanize them—kill them painlessly—so I took them home too. They died, but I believe they might have been saved in the proper kind of facility.

"These two events made me realize that there was a need for a wildlife rehabilitation center in our area where people could bring wildlings to be helped. Most animal shelters are overflowing with pets and just aren't set up to give wildlife the kind of care that's required. They don't have the space, the cages, or the

personnel with enough time, knowledge, and experience to rehabilitate wildlife.''

So Betsy borrowed money and bought an old farmhouse on
ten acres near Ellenville, a country town in the foothills of the
Catskill Mountains in New York State, and moved into it by
herself with her dogs. She began to read books on wildlife and

The farmhouse at Ellenville where Lifeline for Wildlife began

to correspond with people who had personal experience in
rehabilitation. She also applied for the state and federal government permits that are necessary for keeping wild animals or birds.

When we think of wild creatures as being free, that isn't really
so. They live under the protection of the state and federal governments, but it's a curious sort of protection. The state and federal
governments can't protect wildlings against the spread of towns,
suburbs, industrial plants, shopping centers, resorts, and other
human settlements and structures that destroy their habitats and
drive them away. They have no protection against pollution and

pesticides that kill them or ruin their dwellings or food supply. In addition, at certain times of the year, citizens can easily get licenses to hunt and trap them.

Most state parks, all national forests, and half of our wildlife refuges allow hunting or trapping or both. The places where animals and birds can live unmolested become fewer every year.

Some threatened or endangered species, such as bald eagles, are protected by law, though people sometimes kill them anyway. Wildlings that are classified as game are legally (as well as illegally) killed by the hundreds of millions every year for sport or money. Game includes deer, elk, moose, bear, wild cats, ducks, pheasant, quail, and many other creatures.

The wildlife officials of each state decide how many deer, for example, can be killed during a hunting season. They use the word *harvested* instead of *killed,* as if the animals were a crop of vegetables. They usually limit the harvesting of does and fawns to assure that there will be plenty of deer the following year for the hunters to shoot. They cut trees and clear brush so the land can support more deer, even if in doing so they harm the habitat for nongame animals. Recently, in just one year, hunters were allowed to shoot a "surplus" of 185,455 deer in New York State alone. All this is called wildlife management.

On the other hand, people can be arrested for trying to help wild animals or birds. It is illegal to take in wildlife—even to help those creatures that are wounded, sick, or orphaned—without a permit. To obtain one, a person must be certified by both the state and federal governments. Wildlife officials rarely get involved in rehabilitation work themselves. They usually are not concerned with the welfare of individual animals—their aim is to increase the size of target populations.

"I got my license from the state fairly soon, but I still needed one from the federal government to allow me to treat migratory birds," Betsy explains. "One day a man from the U.S. Fish and Wildlife Service showed up at my door to examine my facility and qualifications. He snooped all around, asked a lot of questions, and went away without saying much. I was rather anxious. But a few weeks later, my permit arrived in the mail."

And so, in January 1979, Lifeline for Wildlife was born. At that time the executive director, the staff, the nurse, and the cage cleaner were all one person: Betsy. Many of the wild birds and animals brought to her, however, needed veterinary care. Fortunately, the vet to whom she had always taken her dogs, Dr. Mark Lerman, agreed to treat the wildlife.

Those early days were lonely and difficult. Betsy took in an average of one patient a day. There was a starling, for example, that had been mangled by a cat; it later died in spite of Betsy's care. There was a grouse that had flown into a window and lost an eye. It also died.

"I remember once sitting up in bed all night with a baby raccoon," she relates. "My three dogs were also in bed with me. I was in my nightgown, holding the baby raccoon in my lap. Toward morning, it died. I've never felt so alone and depressed in my life."

But other raccoons lived, and by the end of the year, she had treated three hundred animals, most of whom had responded to her care and survived to be released.

An infant raccoon is weighed . . .

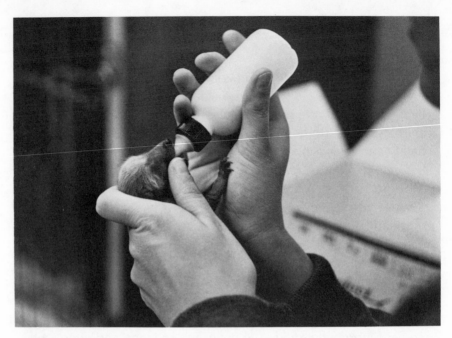

fed, and kissed for good measure.

Betsy's days went something like this: She would get up very early in the morning to take care of the animals at the farm, then drive to Dr. Lerman's veterinary hospital, more than an hour away. At night, she'd come home with boxes of more animals— wildlife that had been brought into the veterinary hospital and been treated, free of charge, by Dr. Lerman. The veterinarian was interested, sympathetic, and helpful.

Some lessons Betsy learned were hard ones. "Once I was treating a baby squirrel at home when the phone rang. I let go of it with one hand to pick up the phone—and did that squirrel bite me! Twelve deep puncture wounds. There was blood all over the kitchen."

There's another incident she knows she'll never forget. It happened on the turnpike when she was driving to an appointment in New York City.

"I was all dressed up—a skirt, makeup, high-heeled boots, the works," Betsy tells. "Suddenly, on the side of the road, I noticed two highway maintenance men standing over a big bird—I could see it was a red-tailed hawk—and they were poking at it with long sticks. I slammed on the brakes, pulled over to the side, leaped out of the car, and ran back, yelling at the top of my voice with all the authority I could muster, 'What are you doing? I'm a professional, I'm a professional—let me handle this!'

"Well, I quickly discovered that the bird had been caught in an illegal snare in a tree. The maintenance men had cut it down and were doing their best to untangle it from the net. But they were wisely afraid of handling it.

"I waded right into the situation. I was so busy trying to help the bird and also prove that I knew how to handle wildlife that I made a bad mistake. I grabbed the hawk the wrong way, and it suddenly gripped my arm with its talons.

"Hawks are raptors—meat eaters—you know. A red-tailed hawk hunts by swooping out of the sky and snatching its prey— a rabbit or mouse, usually—in its talons, which are strong and sharp. Four of the talons went right into my arm about an inch deep and became embedded there. The hawk hung on. Blood spurted from my arm, and I almost fainted from pain.

"The men were horrified. 'Shall we call an ambulance?' one of them gasped. I was convinced I'd be dead by the time an ambulance got there. Also, the pain was simply excruciating—I had to disengage that bird from my body.

"So I grit my teeth and ripped the hawk's talons out of my arm myself. I laid my arm open in the process, and my blood was pouring out, but I managed to get the hawk into a box in my car somehow. Then I wrapped my arm and drove myself to a hospital. I forget how many stitches I had to have. But I've certainly never made a mistake like that again."

Lifeline was growing. More wild animals and birds were coming in. And Betsy knew it would take more than heart, more than just dedication on her part, if Lifeline was going to succeed and meet the need she had set out to fill. From the very beginning, she had planned Lifeline as a fully professional organization, not as her private, solo operation. She wanted it to be a well-staffed, smoothly running, not-for-profit corporation.

Fortunately, she could draw on her experience in running a business, and it began to pay off. She kept careful records and accounts. She set about fund-raising and organized public relations campaigns.

One money-raising scheme she created was Canine and Feline Vacations. She took in dogs and cats whose owners were going on vacation or business trips and needed a place to board them. She guaranteed a homelike atmosphere for the pets, and many owners preferred that to a commercial kennel. The farmhouse began to fill up with dogs who lounged on the worn-out couch and cats who slept on the bed.

Also, Betsy got the idea of creating a program for student interns. She decided to accept a limited number of high school and college students who wanted to live at the farmhouse for a few weeks at a time, pay a small boarding fee, and learn about wild animals and birds while helping to take care of them. So in 1981 she set up and advertised her program.

She immediately hit a snag. So far as the officials in the New York Department of Environmental Conservation (DEC) were concerned, Betsy's taking in wildlings and trying to help them seemed harmless enough. Since many millions of wild creatures are born every year in the state, saving a few thousand which otherwise would die had no real impact on the ecology of the state's wilderness areas and parks.

But having students working to save wildlife was quite another matter. The New York DEC, which has the same function as the variously named fish and game departments in other states, sells hunting, fishing, and trapping licenses. All state wildlife departments get most of their funds this way. And like other state wildlife departments, the New York DEC encourages these so-called sports. The last thing it wanted to see was a project that might influence young people to oppose hunting and trapping.

The DEC officials were suspicious of Betsy's intern program. They apparently began to worry that young people who spent time caring for wildlings and trying to help them might take a negative view of slaughtering them for sport or money.

Armed DEC officers started showing up without warning at the Lifeline farm, often at odd hours, such as seven o'clock in the morning. They informed Betsy that everything she was doing was illegal in spite of her permits. They threatened to close down Lifeline for Wildlife.

"It seemed to me like real harassment," Betsy says indignantly, recalling that period in Lifeline's struggle to survive. "But I wasn't going to let my dreams go down the drain just because these men were trying to intimidate me. I decided to fight back.

"I got an appointment with a powerful senator in the state capital and went to see her. I told her my whole story. She listened very sympathetically and promised to write to the DEC on Lifeline's behalf. I left her office not knowing what to expect.

"But the trouble stopped. I never had any more problems with the DEC. And as a matter of fact, the department officers eventually changed their attitude toward us completely. Today, they not only leave us alone, but they are friendly and cooperative. They often bring us animals or birds. They don't have the time, manpower, or facilities to do what we do, so they look on us as a place to take wildlife or to refer anyone who asks them what to do with an injured or orphaned creature."

A student intern learns how to feed an orphaned fawn.

As for the student interns, soon some sixty young people a year were coming to stay at the farm, a few at a time and for periods that ranged from a week to several months. These students enjoy an intensive experience in the hands-on care of wildlife.

In 1981, Dr. Mark Lerman officially became the medical director of Lifeline, and the first part-time staff members were hired. Two years after Betsy moved into the farmhouse by herself and took care of her first helpless birds and beasts, Lifeline for Wildlife was a firmly established and growing organization.

The founder is very clear about the reasons for the organization's existence and its goals.

"Leaving orphaned and injured wild creatures to die, saying

An intern holds an infant wild animal for the first time.

that this is nature's way of creating a balance, is a cop-out that makes it easy for people to turn their backs and do nothing,'' says Betsy Lewis. ''The balance of nature has already been greatly distorted almost everywhere by the actions of human beings. Pollution, pesticides, habitat destruction—all the adverse effects of civilization—wipe out not only individual creatures but whole species.

''Recently scientists have become deeply concerned about the decline in American forestland, which they believe to be caused mainly by air pollution. When the forests go, all the forest-dwelling birds and animals die too.

''Most of the wildlings brought to us are not sick or injured by

Student interns enjoy supper outdoors at the Ellenville Center. An oversized guest at Canine and Feline Vacations, tethered a few yards away, has dined already but gladly would again. Below: Chow time for a convalescent wildling

A small wild bird, ready to be released, is a source of wonder and delight.

As these interns discover, setting a wild creature free is a high point in wildlife rehabilitation.

natural causes, but by manmade causes. I think that this gives us an even greater obligation to them. Just to ignore the individual animal or bird that needs help is to say that its life has no meaning.

"What does this tell us about ourselves? If a child sees that nobody cares about an injured or orphaned rabbit, for instance, the child concludes that the rabbit's life is of no consequence. If its life is unimportant, the child may then reason, perhaps other lives don't matter either. This kind of thinking brutalizes us, makes us callous.

"By providing a place where people can bring individual wild creatures that need help, we are helping to confirm the value of life. Lifeline's goal is to instill and encourage respect for all life. All wild creatures are welcome here."

3 The Veterinarian

Dr. Mark Lerman stands over the anesthetized form of an infant doe fawn in the operating room of his veterinary hospital. The tiny deer was born with a deformity of her front legs: The tendons are too tight, so the little hooves curl backward under her body. This makes it impossible for her to walk—she can only hobble on her knees. Her mother, probably realizing there was something very wrong with her baby, apparently abandoned her, for when the fawn was found, she was near starvation.

Standing at the operating table and watching Mark are two young people, their faces a study in intense concern and concentration. Light-haired, blue-eyed Nancy Deacon, a Lifeline for Wildlife staff member, gently strokes the unconscious animal's head. Dark, mustached Steve Osofsky, a Harvard student who plans to apply to veterinary college, is spending a semester break helping Mark. Neither says a word as they watch, because Mark is struggling with a difficult job. A well-built, medium-tall man in his late thirties, the veterinarian wears a green surgical coat.

Dr. Lerman knows that the fawn's type of deformity occurs sometimes among hooved animals, and he consulted on the telephone that morning with a horse veterinarian who'd had experience with foals with the same problem. What he is trying to do is to hyperextend the fawn's legs, stretching the tendons so that the legs are straight, and then splint them so that they will remain straight as the baby grows. But he has to be extremely careful not to tear the delicate tendons while he stretches them, going by feel alone.

It's hard to get the splints on tight enough to do any good, and after repeated attempts, Mark realizes that he must put the animal under deeper anesthesia. But now he has difficulty getting the tube for the anesthetic down the fawn's long, narrow little mouth. The room is very quiet as Mark works. With devotion and determination, he is bringing all his skills and experience to help this defenseless baby animal.

Finally he gets the splints secured, and Nancy takes the fawn off the table and lays her gently in a cage in a hospital room with other animals. She will be watched carefully until she is fully conscious.

Mark's next patient is a crow that had been found hopping aimlessly by a roadside, holding up one foot, which looked grotesque. One of its toes had been injured somehow, the blood supply cut off, and gangrene has developed. Mark sees that the toe is dead and that gangrene is beginning to spread up the bird's

Dr. Mark Lerman, having saved this crow's life, is rewarded with a quick nip.

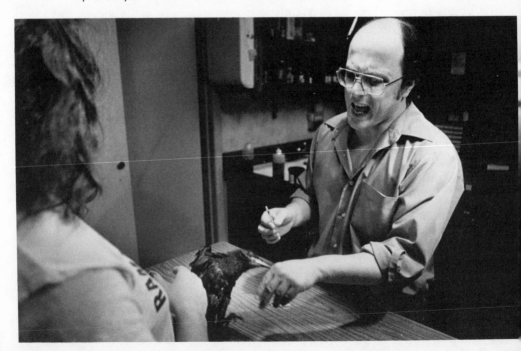

leg, so he amputates the toe cleanly. Then he puts a dressing and bandage on the wound and gives the bird an injection of antibiotics.

"I hope I won't have to take off more than that one toe," he comments. "Birds are beautifully engineered creatures, but very delicate. Before amputating one of their feet, you have to take several things into consideration. Some birds can get along perfectly okay with just one foot. But a falcon, owl, or other raptor, which uses its feet to capture prey, will rarely survive with one foot.

"And the weight of a bird is also a factor. A crow feeds on the ground, eating grain, seeds, and insects, but it is a relatively heavy bird. It would not be able to walk or run if it had only one foot.

"If the time arrives when amputation of this crow's entire foot is necessary to save its life, I'll have to choose among several options. I can amputate the foot and release the bird, hoping that it will survive on its own. I can amputate and attempt to find it a permanent home in a nature museum where it will be cared for for life. Or I can euthanize it. I hope I won't have to make that decision."

Next, Mark tends the very sick female opossum with the mysterious disease, giving her antibiotics and supportive fluids.

"We just don't know enough," he says thoughtfully. Mark is an easygoing and modest person, friendly and curious, always ready to listen. "The field of wildlife veterinary medicine is very new, and there are only a few of us in it. Much of what we do is educated guesswork. If someone who brings us an animal or bird has actually seen it get hurt—shot, hit by a car, attacked by another animal, or whatever—then we know what to do for it. But otherwise, we sometimes can't even tell if it is sick or injured. All we have to start with is a wild creature about which nothing is known except that it needs help—but what kind? In these cases, wildlife veterinary medicine is much like detective work."

On the wall of the operating room is a chart that Mark adds to regularly. It lists the type and amount of anesthetic he has given to various wildlings before surgery, noting the species, weight,

Dr. Lerman, assisted by preveterinary student Steve Osofsky, treats a raccoon with an abscess on its underbelly.

approximate age, and general condition. This valuable information not only guides him with his own wild patients but is shared with other wildlife veterinarians.

"It took me nearly a year to figure out the right amount of anesthetic to give opossums," he remarks. "They can take a lot more, per body weight, than dogs or cats can."

Mark has served on the board of directors of the National Wildlife Rehabilitators Association. Rehabilitators from all parts of the United States meet once a year to get to know one another and to exchange information on all facets of the professional rescue, care, and release of wildlings.

A similar group, the Wildlife Rehabilitation Council, exists mainly on the West Coast, but the two organizations keep in touch and members serve on each other's board of directors. In addition, individual states may have their own organization of rehabilitators.

Sometimes Mark has to treat animals or birds whose legs or paws have been injured in leghold traps. These traps capture a victim, usually by a leg, and hold it tightly so it can't get away. The trap shuts off the blood flow to the limb, and after a while, gangrene sets in. Meanwhile, of course, the creature suffers intensely from terror, exposure, hunger, and thirst.

Trappers and state wildlife officers point out that most states have laws requiring trappers to visit their traps daily or every few days. But there is absolutely no way to enforce such laws or to know if they are obeyed. Even if a trapper checks his trap daily, twenty-four hours is a long time for the captured animal or bird to endure the torture, which ends only when the trapper eventually comes along and kills it, usually by clubbing or stomping it to death.

Because the leghold trap is so cruel, caring people in many countries around the world have succeeded in getting it banned. But in the United States, this trap is outlawed in only a few states. Bills to ban it have been introduced in some state legislatures, but most haven't been passed. Apparently, most voters are unaware of, or indifferent to, the suffering caused by the leghold trap; if they thought about it, they might insist that this trap be made illegal in their state.

"Sometimes an animal, in its pain and panic, will chew off its own leg to get away, leaving just its paw in the trap," Betsy Lewis points out. "Females with nursing babies are especially likely to do this. Such an animal may die from infection or loss of blood.

If it is a predator, it will have enormous difficulty hunting food to stay alive. Once in a while, these three-legged animals are found by kindhearted people and brought to wildlife rehabilitators."

A trap will, of course, snap shut on any creature that steps into it, so it is not unusual for pet dogs or cats to be caught, or wildlings that trappers consider "trash" because their pelts are not valuable.

Sometimes birds are caught also. "A leading cause of injury to eagles, by the way, is the leghold trap," says Mark. "Their legs have only two veins. The trap shuts off the blood supply, and gangrene results.

"Rehabilitators urge people not to simply liberate an animal or bird they take out of a leghold trap, even if it seems unharmed," Mark continues. "Whatever part of its body was held by the trap may be gangrenous, and the wildling will soon die as the decay spreads. It is important to bring any creature that has been in a trap to a rehabilitator or veterinarian for examination and treatment as quickly as possible."

Now Steve brings in a male baby raccoon that needs Mark's attention. The animal was found suffering, too sick to move, on a path in the woods. When Mark first examined him, he felt an enlarged bladder and noticed that the little raccoon's penis had an extremely narrow opening that had become clogged. The raccoon couldn't urinate and would have soon died.

After Mark relieved the young animal by unclogging him, he operated and enlarged the opening in the penis. Now, the incision has healed, and all that has to be done today is to remove the few tiny stitches around the edges. Steve holds the squirming baby on the table. Mark makes a couple of quick snips with surgical scissors, and the stitches are out. The raccoon now will be able to urinate normally.

Mark gives him a dose of worm medicine before Steve puts him back in his cage. "Virtually all wild creatures—animals and birds alike—are severely parasitized. There's a safe new drug for worms, so I give it routinely now," says the veterinarian.

Someone has just brought in a day-old raccoon who is cold

A little raccoon, headed for the treatment room at the hospital, hides its eyes in fright.

"See, that wasn't so bad," Steve comforts the raccoon later.

from exposure. The tiny creature looks quite dead, but Mark and Betsy wrap it in a heating pad.

"We'll tube-feed it as soon as possible, but we have to warm it up first," Mark explains. "When an animal is this cold, the enzymes in its body aren't functioning, so it wouldn't be able to digest food."

How can Dr. Mark Lerman afford to spend so much of his time treating wildlife, for whom nobody pays the bills? He does it by working long hours, so that he can carry on his regular small-animal veterinary practice with pet dogs and cats and still give wildlife all the time necessary.

"I like working with exotic animals, the earth's most unusual creatures," he says. "But instead of treating captive tigers in a zoo or parrots in a pet store, I'd rather care for animals and birds who have no one to help them and who can be set free when they get well.

"I suppose some people might find it hard to justify the time and money we spend treating and caring for these wild creatures, the common and the rare alike. But we do it out of respect for their individual lives.

"We once took in a great blue heron, a huge migratory wading bird, who ate seventy dollars' worth of fish a week," he recalls with a smile and a shrug. "We kept him several months, until he was well, but he couldn't fly again, so we gave him to the Bronx Zoo."

Mark, who received his veterinary degree from Cornell University, in Ithaca, New York, had been in small-animal practice in Rockland County for nearly ten years when he met Betsy. It was through her that Mark became interested in treating wildlife. Soon after she established her organization, she asked him to be Lifeline's vet.

"I see a lot of hope in our work," he says. "I think that those of us involved in wildlife rehabilitation can help change the attitudes of other people toward wild animals and birds. We do it by example. We show that we consider these creatures important and worth saving, the ordinary and unattractive ones as well as those that are rare and beautiful.

"If the public will just go 5 percent of the way, by not leaving helpless wildlings to die, we will go the remaining 95 percent to try to save their lives. If people will only bring the injured, sick, and orphaned creatures to us, or call us to come and get them, we'll do our best to rehabilitate them and return them to the wild.

"By providing this service and encouraging the public to use it, I think we fulfill a much needed obligation. We certainly help individual animals and birds, but just as important, we help people to be compassionate."

The next day, the fawn with the deformed legs dies. In spite of all the medical and nursing care she got, the damaging effects of her severe disability could not be reversed.

The crow looks good. With luck, its foot will heal and become healthy, and soon the bird can be set free to live the normal life of a crow.

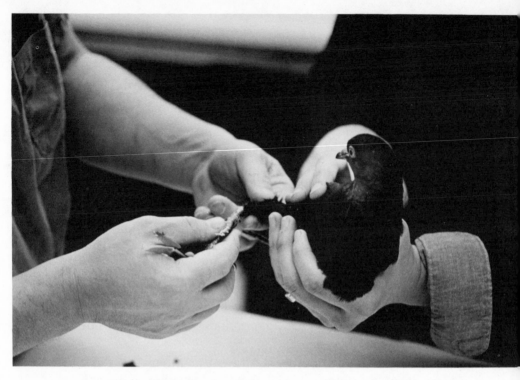

A pigeon with a broken leg is examined by Lifeline's vet. Below: Betsy and Mark check out a recovered hawk to be sure it's ready for release.

The opossum is still hanging on to her life with plenty of help. No decision will be made about her future unless she gets worse. If her illness can't be diagnosed and treated, and it becomes obvious that she is failing, Mark will euthanize her painlessly by injection.

The male baby raccoon is squealing for food, pacing back and forth in his cage. He'll be sent to the Ellenville Center and kept with other baby raccoons. When they're all old enough to be on their own, they will be taken to a safe, secluded wilderness area and released together.

The newborn raccoon, still on a heating pad, has made it so far and is being given regular nourishment by tube until it is old enough to take a bottle.

And Mark is busy with the new day's wildlife patients.

Lifeline keeps a daily record of basic information on every patient: Did it have surgery? What treatment? Is it convalescing well? Was euthanasia necessary? Has it been released?

4 Rescues

Judy Lapine, a tall, slender woman with light brown hair and large blue eyes, stands at the front of a high school classroom, speaking to a group of students. She talks about the animals at Lifeline for Wildlife and shows slides. She stresses the reasons that these animals do not make suitable pets and why it is against the law in New York State and many other states for the public to keep them.

"Whenever you find a helpless wild animal, especially a baby, it's very tempting to take it home and raise it as a pet," Judy says. "The animal may be a great pet when it's very young, but as it grows up and reaches sexual maturity, its wild instincts emerge, and the animal will become restless, destructive, extremely unhappy, and even unfriendly.

"Wild animals are not like domestic animals. Puppies and kittens, if they're loved and well treated, become more and more gentle, tame, affectionate, and docile as they grow up. Our homes are their natural habitat.

"Wild animals, on the other hand, are just the opposite. While they may be tame and loving as infants, they become less and less petlike as they become adults. Our homes are definitely not their natural habitat, and it is really cruel to keep them.

"The best thing to do for any sick, injured, or orphaned wild animal or bird is to take it to a wildlife rehabilitation center and give it a chance for life. Then it can be returned to the wild and live a normal life as soon as possible."

Judy looks at the faces of her listeners and hopes that they will think about what she has told them. They seem to be paying attention, but will they remember? Lifeline, like others involved in wildlife rehabilitation, believes that this type of humane education is important. Judy speaks regularly at schools, clubs, and scout troops—wherever there is an interest.

After lecturing at the high school, Judy continues on to New York City to pick up two dogs whose owners are going on vacation and are sending them to Canine and Feline Vacations, Lifeline's pet-sitting service at the Ellenville Center. The dogs bounce around in the back of the car, shedding hair on the seat and smearing the windows with their noses as they gaze out. Judy's car always shows evidence of animals—paw prints, a few feathers, a leash, a carrying cage, a drinking bowl, a blanket. She is indifferent to the condition of her car. What is important to her is that it serves to transport animals, wild or domestic, whenever it's needed.

Judy Lapine has been a model and a housewife, and she was over thirty years old before she went to college. Today she lives with her teenage son and daughter plus their pets—two dogs, three cats, two hamsters, two gerbils, twelve ducks, two goats, two geese, and five rabbits. She seems to have arranged her life successfully according to her true priorities.

Judy is a full associate at Lifeline and actually could be called

Judy and Dr. Lerman have a conference over an infant squirrel.

Infant animals must defecate after eating. In the wild, a mother animal stimulates a baby by licking it, but in Lifeline's clinic, this task is imitated with a cotton swab. Below: Judy medicates an abscess on the throat of a little squirrel while staff member Cindy Simpson takes notes.

general factotum—someone who does everything. She helps run the office, answering calls and meeting people who come in with wildlife. She can also rescue a creature in trouble or nurse a sick one. Calm and capable, she is a valued colleague to Betsy Lewis and Mark Lerman.

Sometimes Lifeline is called upon to remove perfectly healthy wild animals who simply happen to be someplace where they're not wanted.

One day in late spring, a woman telephones the office. "There are wild geese in a pond where our children swim," she complains. "They might poison the water. We want them out of that pond before summer—can you get rid of them for us?"

Promising to help, Betsy hangs up the phone. "Some people simply can't accept wild creatures as neighbors," she says with a sigh. "Judy, I can't leave the office today, and the assistants are needed in the hospital. Would you mind going with Marc Payne to do something about those geese?"

"Sure, I'll go," says Judy, putting on her jacket. Marc Payne, a black-bearded man in his late twenties, is manager of the Ellenville Center, supervising the care of the wildlife there. He has come to the hospital today to pick up animals that are well enough or old enough to be moved to the outdoor cages, where they will stay until they can be released.

Judy and Marc put pole nets in Judy's car and head for the location the caller indicated. It is a large pond, and a family of Canada geese—parents and three goslings—are idling along one bank.

"There's no way these few geese could contaminate this pond," Judy observes, surveying the scene. "But we'd better relocate them anyway."

"The parents won't fly away and leave the babies," says Marc. "If we can capture them, it will be easy to catch the goslings. Let's herd them down to one end of the pond. You take that side, and I'll work from here."

He wades into the water, holding the net behind him. But the adult geese, suspicious, swim away from him. Then, seeing Judy on the other bank, they move toward the shallow water at one end, the little ones trailing along behind. Judy and Marc wade after them, slowly and quietly. The bottom of the pond is mucky and slippery.

Finally they realize it's now or never. Quickly they close in on the birds and swipe at them with the nets. They miss. Judy, who can't swim, falls into the water, yelping. Marc also loses his footing and thrashes about in the water. The geese flap and honk and squawk, swimming away as fast as they can.

"Let's keep trying—we can't get any wetter," says Judy, wringing out the edge of her jacket over her muddy jeans.

Nearly two hours later, Judy and Marc are soaked through to their skins and covered with mud, but the male and female geese are secured in nets. The bewildered goslings are picked up and put in a box. Shivering, Judy and Marc drive the family to a larger, more secluded body of water some miles away and set them free. Still indignant, the big gray and black birds paddle off, followed by their babies.

Marc Payne worked at Lifeline as a volunteer for a year before joining the staff as manager of the Ellenville facility. He had grown up in the area, surrounded by pets, and had worked in a pet store when he was a teenager. It bothered him that sometimes the pet-store owner would simply throw surplus living creatures, such as lizards and frogs, into the trash can, but his feelings about animals were not fully formed then. Two years of college out West found him still seeking what he wanted to do with his life.

"College biology classes, forestry classes, and the like are all geared toward the economic or consumer value of nature to people," he reflects today. "And all the animals we studied were dead. The attitude seemed to be: Go out and catch them, kill them, and then study them.

"So I quit school, came back home, and got a job with an animal dealer in New Jersey who imported exotic animals from all over the world for zoos, laboratories, and collectors. I was so glad to be working with living animals, I didn't face the fact that I was engaged in a cruel activity. These captive wild animals were headed not for freedom but for the worst kind of existence, or even death.

"Then I worked for a veterinarian who was himself a big-game hunter. I got hands-on experience with animals in both jobs, but I'm appalled now when I think that I was working for people who exploited wild animals or killed them for sport.

"That's why I love my work in wildlife rehabilitation. Having been part of the other side, I especially appreciate what we do. Our work is to conserve, not destroy. I believe animals have intrinsic rights—they're here for a reason, not just to serve us. They feel and hurt much as we do. If I trap or capture them, it's for their own ultimate benefit. And the high point of it all is to release them!"

One beautiful spring day, Marc is again asked to remove some animals that are simply in the wrong place. Like the request involving the geese, this is not a report of an injured animal but of animals that someone has decided are a nuisance. Raccoons this time—a mother with four babies.

According to the people who called Lifeline, a mother raccoon has taken up residence under their back porch every year for nearly a decade. The animal apparently thinks that this sheltered spot is a good place to have her babies, especially since it's near a steady food supply—the neighborhood garbage cans. But the neighbors have complained so much about the mess she makes —overturning garbage cans and rummaging through them to pick and choose what she wants—that the people under whose house she is living have decided something has to be done about her.

Marc and Joe Schneider, a college student working at Lifeline for the summer, drive to the house and discover that they can reach the nest easily from the basement. The first thing they do is to spread a large plastic sheet on the basement floor.

"Raccoons sometimes defecate out of fear when they're first captured," Marc comments. "No point in messing up the basement."

He has brought with him a long pole with a noose on the end, called a come-along or catch-pole, which animal control officers often use in capturing stray dogs and cats. Counting on the mother raccoon not to leave her babies and run, he carefully reaches in under the porch with the come-along. Naturally, he can't slip it over her head and tighten it around her neck, because that would choke her.

Most people would have had a hard time getting the noose around her chest and under her front legs, but Marc accomplishes this in seconds and lifts the surprised big animal painlessly out of the nest and into a carrying cage on the basement floor before she has a chance to panic. She sits in the cage glaring at everyone, but doesn't struggle or cry.

Then Marc and Joe reach in by hand and lift the four babies out from under the porch one by one. The largest baby hisses at them. The men put them in a carrying cage right next to the mother.

"She won't get upset as long as she can see her babies," says Marc.

Just then, two little boys from next door come running in to see the wild animals that have been captured. They squeal and jump around, showing no sympathy for the frightened animals. In fact, there's a strong undercurrent of violence in their behavior.

"Are you going to kill them?" one child asks excitedly. If a slaughter is going to take place, this boy clearly wants to watch.

Marc explains that of course he is not going to kill them. Instead, he will take the raccoons to a deserted wooded area miles away and set them free where they won't bother anybody.

"Oh," says the boy with obvious disappointment.

The couple whose house the animals had nested under are sympathetic and concerned—after all, they called Lifeline rather than an exterminating service, which most likely would have killed the whole family.

"We'll take them to the clinic, and our veterinarian will check them over to be sure they're healthy and vaccinate them against distemper," Marc assures the couple. "Tomorrow, they'll go right out—we'll take them to a wilderness area and release them."

Sometimes nuisance-control permits are issued by state authorities to persons unqualified to handle wildlife. Exterminators, for example, often see their job as merely one of getting rid of nuisance animals by killing them. Raccoons are especially vulnerable because their pelts are worth money.

Chimney sweeps, people who specialize in cleaning chimneys, are often called to get rid of wild animals or birds that have nested in flues. Some chimney sweeps act like exterminators. Yet others have shown up at Lifeline with creatures they have found in the course of their work. One chimney sweep even rushed into Lifeline's hospital with a little raccoon that apparently had been caught in a lighted fireplace and burned before it could escape.

The next day, early in the evening, Marc and Joe drive the mother raccoon and her four babies far into a state park. They leave the car and carry the cages deep into the quiet woods. The evening is cloudy and cool; now and then, a bird calls as it flies to its nest for the night. Wild flowers have pushed up here and there through the forest floor. The mother raccoon sniffs the fragrant air; the babies stare about them. The young men set the cages down on the ground and open them.

The mother raccoon lumbers off at once, acting happy to be free, never knowing, of course, how fortunate she and her babies are. The little raccoons scramble after her, and she pauses long enough for them to catch up. Marc watches them go with satisfaction.

"I've only had one case where the mother took off without waiting for her babies," he says. "The babies screamed and screamed for her. We went away and then came back, but she hadn't returned for them. Since by then it was obvious she wasn't going to, we brought the babies back to Ellenville and kept them along with the other young raccoons until they were grown."

Before they leave the release site, Marc and Joe do the mother raccoon and her offspring another favor. They leave an empty wooden box on its side for them to nest in if they need it. Otherwise, the mother and her brood might have to walk and walk for miles trying to find a suitable hollow log. The men also leave a few days' supply of food. After that, the animals will be on their own, as they should be.

The people who had called Lifeline to rescue the raccoons

A chimney sweep brings baby raccoons to Lifeline. Below: Mark examines the foot of a raccoon who got caught in a hot chimney.

under their porch, and the little boys who acted as if they would gladly have seen them clubbed to death, present a contrast in attitude that wildlife rehabilitators continually confront.

Marc tells of a snapping turtle that had been brought to the Lifeline hospital injured and near death. The sympathetic person who brought it in had rescued it from a group of youngsters in a public park who had cornered it and were trying to drive a spike through its shell. Dr. Lerman repaired the shell, and the turtle recovered. After several weeks, Marc released it on the shore of a lake in a secluded place.

Marc Payne and an intern carry a raccoon to freedom.

Marc and the intern scatter food for the animal.

The raccoon is eager to leave but may come back later for the food.

Lifeline and other rehabilitators see many, many examples of human cruelty inflicted on animals, quite often by ignorant and insensitive children. Yet, animals and birds that need help are frequently brought to Lifeline by children. Some children learn respect for animals from their parents. Other kids seem to be born with it.

"It makes me feel good to know there are some people out there who respect the lives of wild creatures," Marc Payne says. "And I think it makes them feel good to know we're here."

5 Caring People

"I'm not a joiner and I never volunteered for anything in my life," says Carol Maloney, a trim, blonde young woman driving along a suburban road. "I'd found some orphaned baby rabbits, very young ones, and as I'd heard about Lifeline for Wildlife, I took them there. My baby rabbits died—I've since learned that if rabbits are orphaned when they're under two weeks of age, they usually don't survive no matter how much care they're given by people. But I was so impressed with the people at Lifeline and their attitude toward animals that I wanted to be part of it. So I joined, first as a volunteer, and now I'm on the staff one full day a week.

"I love animals, nature, the outdoors. I have my own horse, and I work in a plant nursery. Helping wildlife fits right in with the rest of my life."

A woman had called Lifeline to report that a duck in a nearby lake had lost part of its beak and couldn't feed. Carol is on her way to pick up the woman, and together they are going to attempt to capture the duck and bring it to Lifeline's hospital to see what can be done for it.

Dawn, the woman who called, is waiting for Carol anxiously. The two women then continue on to the lake.

"This is a Peking duck—in other words, a domestic, not a wild duck," Dawn tells Carol. "I've been feeding him for over seven years. He was put in this lake, along with four others, when they

A good sign—this wild baby rabbit is beginning to eat. Its littermate died, but this one will probably live to grow up and be released.

were all just ducklings. It was right after Easter—I suppose they had been somebody's idea of a cute Easter present, and after the holiday, the novelty wore off, as usual, and they were just dumped.

"One by one, they were killed—by snapping turtles, dogs, fishermen, whatever. A female who had been this duck's mate died only last year. She'd been attacked and badly hurt, perhaps by stray dogs, perhaps by people, and by the time we could catch her, it was too late. This duck is the lone survivor of the little Easter ducks. A local man and I take turns feeding him and the wild ducks regularly."

It is a large lake, surrounded by trees but not isolated from human habitation. The road follows its contours for some distance. Carol pulls off and parks the car.

Out in the middle of the lake, a large beautiful white duck can be seen paddling around with a flock of smaller brown and gray wild ducks. Dawn calls to them. The Peking duck obviously recognizes her and swims right over to the bank. Dawn offers bread, tossing it onto the water. The white duck tries hard to eat, poking unsuccessfully at the bits of bread floating on the water. Now Dawn and Carol can see that his entire upper beak is missing, exposing his tongue. No matter how hard he tries, he can't seize the food. The wild ducks, wary but appreciative, circle around in the water gobbling up the bread.

"It's illegal to fish in this lake, but people come and fish anyway," Dawn says bitterly. "I suspect that's how he lost his beak. He probably got tangled in somebody's fishing line, and the person pulled or cut his beak off to free the line."

Carol takes a pole net and hides in the tall bushes at the side of the lake while Dawn tries to lure the duck onto the narrow shore. He is so hungry that he almost comes out of the water, but each time he loses his nerve and hangs back, staying near the shore and trying to eat the pieces of bread that Dawn tosses to him. After years of living with wild ducks, he himself is quite wild. He has learned to keep his distance from people, even from someone like Dawn, who is a source of food and has never tried to harm him.

Carol realizes she'll have only one chance to capture the Peking duck, because if she scares him, he'll swim away and won't return. In a lake the size of this one, it would be necessary to pursue him in a boat. Patiently, she waits and waits her chance. Dawn quacks to the duck as she has always done and keeps offering him bread.

The wild ducks finish feeding and paddle off in a leisurely way. The Peking duck lingers, still trying to eat. Finally, he seems to get discouraged, for he retreats farther out into the lake, though from time to time he comes back in response to Dawn's coaxing. Nearly two hours have passed.

Carol, crouched in the bushes, decides she has to make a move. The next time the duck ventures near the shore, she lunges into the water and swings the net at him. The net comes close, but misses. The duck takes off, and in seconds he is way out in the middle of the lake.

"Well, that's it for now," says Carol regretfully. "He won't come back today."

Disheartened, the two women depart, leaving the injured duck beyond reach and still hungry. Back at the Lifeline office, Carol explains to Betsy what happened. Another plan will have to be devised.

Early the next morning, however, Dawn telephones. "My husband caught the duck last night," she reports. "He used to be a volunteer fireman, so he gathered up a bunch of his friends from the fire department, and they went out in boats with big nets. It took half the night, but they got him." She drops off the duck at Lifeline on her way to work.

Later in the morning, Dr. Mark Lerman examines him at the hospital. Everybody gathers around, hoping for good news. Mark, however, doesn't look cheerful.

"The mutilation is too severe," he explains. "The upper beak has been pulled away from the frontal bones, clear up to the sinuses. I had hoped to be able to fashion a plastic beak and attach it to whatever was left of the duck's own beak, but there's nothing to attach an artificial beak to. It's hopeless." He turns away in disappointment.

There is no alternative but to euthanize the bird. "You can't put him back in the lake and let him starve to death," Betsy tells Dawn over the phone as gently as she can. "That would be cruel, as you know. Even if he remained in captivity, he couldn't eat. The kindest thing to do for this bird is to painlessly put him to sleep."

Dawn weeps as if she has lost a good friend.

It must have taken an extremely hard yank to pull the duck's beak clear out of its face. Some person, probably fishing illegally in the lake, with one impatient and vicious act cost an innocent being its life.

When Valerie Plesko, another former volunteer who has become a staff member, comes into the hospital after school, she asks about the Peking duck. Her face falls when she hears the news. Everyone at Lifeline has been concerned about the starving bird.

"When I first joined Lifeline, I had a hard time handling death," Valerie says. "I remember a raccoon that I really put my heart into saving. Dr. Lerman was trying to pull her through, but she had distemper and was anemic. I asked my mother to make a real nourishing chicken soup—with lots of meat, carrots, potatoes, and other good stuff in it. I brought it to the hospital. The raccoon ate the soup and seemed to enjoy it, but later she died anyway." The attractive high school student pauses, searching for just the right words to express her thoughts.

"You get your rewards from the ones that live, and fortunately most do."

Valerie thinks she might want to become a veterinarian or a veterinary technician. In addition to helping clean cages and feed the animals, she writes up a short medical report on each creature's condition for Dr. Lerman.

"Every one of us is important here," Valerie continues earnestly. "Nobody is ever looked down on. We're all here to save lives—and when the animals live, that's a real turn-on!"

This must be the secret that makes one young woman pitch in every week to do whatever is needed to help the animals and keep the rehabilitation work going, even if it means wading fully clothed into a cold lake to try to catch a duck. It must be what inspires another young woman to come in after a day of school, roll up her sleeves, and clean messy cages, knowing that some animals will die no matter how much care they are given and that even those who live will leave forever as soon as they're able.

Betsy Lewis is a strong role model, a demanding and persuasive leader. She insists that Lifeline function not as a dilettante—that is, amateurish—operation, but as a fully professional organization. She feels that only by setting high standards and enforcing them can she make Lifeline effective.

For this reason, as soon as a volunteer proves competent and dependable, he or she is given increased responsibility and put on a salary, small though it may be. This is partly a way of showing appreciation and encouragement and of keeping morale high. It is also consistent with Betsy's seriousness of purpose.

Shari Stahl is a volunteer who soon went on salary, not part-time like many of the staff, but full-time. Tall, black-haired Shari had been attending a community college, majoring in psychology, when she heard about Lifeline for Wildlife and decided to volunteer. Now she not only participates in the hands-on care of the animals, but helps in the office. She uses the computer, which stores financial and membership details as well as complete medical records on every animal and bird treated at the hospital.

"I discovered that wildlife rehabilitation gave me an opportunity to put into action feelings I'd had for a long time," Shari says. "This work makes me feel I'm helping the world—animals and people alike. It seems to me that people have lost a lot of their compassion, their respect for the earth. Wildlife rehabilitation helps keep such good qualities alive. Through my work here, I feel that I'm doing something about my beliefs instead of just thinking about them."

Shari remembers an experience she had two or three months after she began volunteering at Lifeline.

"I was insecure and inexperienced, so I'd been sticking close to Betsy, trying to learn as much as I could by watching and listening to her," Shari relates. "It was spring, and the hospital was full of baby birds that needed continual feedings. One night somebody had to stay late and feed them, and Betsy asked me. So there I was, in charge, all alone.

"A woman brought in two very tiny baby birds. They were so young they had only a little down on them, and their eyes weren't even open. I put them in a box on a heating pad and watched them carefully. Toward midnight, one of them died. I was extremely upset because I thought it must be my fault.

"The next day, I rushed up to Betsy and cried, 'Tell me what I did wrong! Teach me, so this won't happen again!' Betsy explained to me that in all probability nothing could have saved that little bird. She made me feel better. And the other one lived, so I must have done something right."

That same spring, Shari was carrying fifteen credits at college, working at a pizza parlor, doing volunteer counseling at school, and working at Lifeline.

"I was pulled in so many directions, and so exhausted, that I had to get my priorities straight," she says. "I felt that wildlife rehabilitation was what I wanted to do for the rest of my life. So I quit everything else, went on staff full-time, and now I feel totally happy and fulfilled. Someday I might want marriage and children, but I'm only twenty, so I don't have to think about that just yet."

The intervention of the caring people in wildlife rehabilitation can only give wild creatures borrowed time, for sooner or later, virtually all will fall victim to one or another of the many dangers that surround them. Life for wild animals and birds is hard and should not be romanticized. It is not like a scene in a Walt Disney cartoon or on a sentimental greeting card. Even in the few places where they are not hunted or trapped, wildlings must continually struggle to survive the ordinary hazards of nature—storms, drought, floods, disease, injuries, and predators. In addition, they are constantly driven from their habitats by human interference. And millions fall victim to pesticides and pollution. But they are entitled to every chance for their short lives.

Shari says she'll never forget the first time she released an animal.

"Another girl and I were releasing an adult raccoon who was ready to be on his own," she recalls, her voice warm with good feelings at the memory. "We were in a state park and knew there were other raccoons in the area. It was a beautiful day, with sunlight slanting through the trees. The forest was very quiet. Two fawns leaped across the path ahead of us. We set down the cage, opened it, and the raccoon stepped out. He gazed about him. Then he looked up at us—looked me in the eye for several long seconds, almost as if to say, 'This is where I belong. Thank you.' And he took off into the woods with that funny little gallop raccoons have."

And that's the bottom line—the lives of wild animals and birds are valuable to them. This profound belief is what keeps people working at Lifeline and at other rehabilitation centers all over the country. It's what wildlife rehabilitation is all about.

Marc uses a catch-pole to transfer an adult raccoon, too wild to handle, to a lighter cage. Below: Out the raccoons go, with Lifeline staffers Ria Schwartz and Diane Wallburg, to a state park.

The raccoons are released one at a time. Below: "Your friend went that way," Ria and Diane tell one raccoon who is looking for the other.

But the second raccoon is hungry and decides to have a meal of the food Ria and Diane have scattered on the ground. Below: The raccoon is free to run into the woods or climb a tree.

6 Valuable Lives

Marc Payne wraps the fawn in a blanket and lifts her into the arms of Mary Catherine Cupp, a high school student who is visiting the Ellenville Center and who has gone with Marc on this errand of mercy. Mary Catherine sits in the backseat of the car with the fawn.

"Try to keep her calm so she won't get upset and thrash about," Marc advises. The little animal is very frightened. She has endured a terrifying twelve hours or more. She was harassed by dogs, separated from her mother, and chased onto some people's property. In her frenzy and confusion, she ran up against the house and backed into a large exhaust fan in the wall. She has several cuts on her body from the fan.

The couple who lives in the house rescued the fawn and called the local SPCA, which in turn telephoned Lifeline for Wildlife. It took Marc over an hour to drive to the house.

Marc thanks the couple and starts back toward Ellenville. The fawn lies quietly on Mary Catherine's lap, exhausted.

Suddenly, as Marc rounds a curve, he notices an animal lying in the middle of the highway. Slowing down, he sees that it is a woodchuck, trying feebly to move. Marc is anxious to get the fawn to the farm as soon as possible, but the woodchuck will surely get hit again and again by cars if it's left where it is.

Marc pulls off to the side of the road and gets out. Mary Catherine stays in the car with the fawn. "Be careful, Marc," she says nervously. Traffic is coming fast.

Marc carefully picks up an orphaned fawn someone has reported.
Harassed by dogs, the fawn has some cuts and bruises on her body.
Below: Mary Catherine tries to comfort the frightened animal.

Marc considers the situation: how to rescue the animal before it is run over, without getting hit himself? The road is too narrow to allow him to stop in the middle while he picks up the woodchuck. He decides he'll have to take the risk and make a run for it.

He waits until there is a little opening in the traffic, then dashes across the road, stooping in the middle and making a grab for the animal as he passes it. He misses.

Standing on the other side, Marc feels his adrenaline rising. There is no letup in the traffic. Then he sees another gap and thinks he can make it. This time as he passes the woodchuck, he scoops it up and gets across the road without a second to spare.

"Good job," breathes Mary Catherine as he returns to the car carrying the animal. "I was watching out the back window, and when you missed the first time, I couldn't look anymore."

Below: *An injured woodchuck lies in the middle of a busy road.*

Opposite, from top to bottom: *Marc's first attempt to rescue it fails, and he has to dash to safety. Mission incomplete. Got it!*

The woodchuck doesn't appear to be crushed anywhere on its body, but seems dazed. Marc lays it in a box on the floor of the car and continues on to Ellenville.

Several student interns come out to the car as he parks under a tree. "I think we should put the fawn in seclusion and let her

A dazed woodchuck regards its rescuer.

calm down a little before we take her on to the hospital," Marc tells them. "She may go into shock if we do any more to her now."

The interns stand back as Marc takes the baby animal from Mary Catherine's arms and carries her into the barn. Like all fawns, she is an enchanting little creature, but the students know better than to follow and watch her.

Marc carries the fawn into the barn at Ellenville.

Marc washes the fawn's wounds quickly with clean water from the faucet and then puts her in an out-of-the-way spot, covering her cage with a tarpaulin. He plans to offer her milk formula from a baby bottle, but right now it is more important to leave her in peace and quiet for a while.

Marc goes back to his car to tend to the woodchuck. But when he looks in the box, it's empty!

"Hey—did anybody move the woodchuck?" he yells. But all the interns have returned to their chores—there is nobody around. Ria Schwartz, the assistant manager of the Ellenville Center and Marc's assistant, comes down from the porch where she had been doing some paperwork.

"Could it have simply walked off?" she asks. The car door had accidentally been left open after Marc removed the fawn.

"But that woodchuck was out cold!" replies Marc. "I thought it would stay that way for a while." Marc and Ria search the grass and bushes for a long time. No woodchuck is to be found.

"I guess it came to while I was busy with the fawn and decided not to wait around," Marc finally decides. "Well, if it was in good enough shape to climb out of the box and take off so completely, it must have been okay."

So the wildlife population at the farm is increased by only one animal instead of two this afternoon.

The following morning, the fawn drinks a baby bottle of milk formula before she is driven to the hospital. Dr. Lerman discovers that, fortunately, the cuts from the blower fan are fairly superficial. Eventually, the animal will be brought back to the farm to convalesce, and later in the summer, when she is well, she'll be taken to a protected (no hunting) wilderness area and released.

Lifeline for Wildlife always releases animals in areas where hunting and trapping are prohibited. Though most state parks nationwide are open to these activities, there are several within

Opposite, from top to bottom: *Marc puts the fawn in a secluded, covered cage and removes the collar that the people who found her had put on her. Judy prepares to give the fawn a bottle of milk formula. The animal drinks eagerly.*

driving distance of Ellenville where animals can be given their freedom in relative safety, protected at least from bullets, arrows, and traps.

Marc tells about another deer that was at the farm a summer ago which had to be released right on the spot at the Ellenville Center. This was a fully grown yearling buck that had been hit by a car and was found wandering, still stunned and suffering from a bad wound at the end of his back. Dr. Lerman had to amputate the animal's tail. It took about two weeks for the wound to heal completely, and during that time the deer was kept in a secluded compound because he was so afraid of human beings and so frantic to be free. While fawns are usually docile and gentle, full-grown wild deer are not. The staff and interns limited their activity around the animal as much as possible because he was so distressed by people.

"When it came time to release him, there was no way we could capture that buck, get him into a car, and transport him to another place," Marc explains. "He was big enough to be dangerous, and also he might have died from sheer stress. So the only thing to do was simply to open the gate to his compound.

"He went through it like a locomotive. But oddly enough, instead of disappearing over the hill in a streak, he stopped running, looked around, and began to browse on the front lawn. He took his time. Finally, he strolled off into the woods as if nothing had happened.

"There's no question but that releasing an animal you've cared for is the high point of wildlife rehabilitation," continues Marc, leaning against the railing on the porch of the farmhouse and reflecting on his work. "But there are other rewards too. Just being around the animals and watching them is satisfying. I liked taking care of a great horned owl we had, even though I never did get the chance to see him released."

The owl had been shot. Someone had found him huddled on a railroad track and brought him to the Lifeline hospital, where Dr. Lerman pinned his badly fractured wing. When the huge,

A starling about to be released complains about being held. Below: Marc shows interns the right way to release a bird.

MARK LERMAN, D.V.M.
Both have been up all night: Whisper because owls are nocturnal, and Marc because Whisper hooted loudly and kept him awake.

powerful raptor was well enough, he was brought to convalesce in a large outdoor flight cage at Ellenville.

"We named him Whisper," says Marc with a wry smile. "What a voice he had. For the first week or so, he kept us all awake at night. Another owl discovered him—a wild owl that would come and sit in a tree alongside Whisper's cage—and the two would screech and hoot at each other for hours. Nobody in the farmhouse got any sleep."

Whisper stayed for about two months. Even though he was

kept in Lifeline's forty-foot flight cage, Betsy realized he would need to exercise his wings gradually in full flight before he could safely be allowed to be on his own. Great horned owls have a wing spread of two to three feet.

So Betsy approached a raptor rehabilitator, who could exercise the big owl with falconry equipment. This allows a bird to fly aloft on a long line, looking rather like a kite, with a person on the ground holding the other end of the line and controlling it. The specialist agreed to take Whisper and release him when he was ready, so Marc never did have the satisfaction of seeing the owl he had cared for fly away free.

Birds like Whisper—the raptors, which include owls, hawks, falcons, and eagles—have been slaughtered relentlessly since the very beginnings of this country. They've been shot, trapped, and poisoned, their nests destroyed. Why? Not because people feel sorry for the birds and small mammals that these birds kill to feed themselves. Some farmers do complain that raptors steal their chickens, but hunters hate these birds generally because raptors kill game birds, such as pheasant and quail, that the hunters themselves like to shoot for sport and gourmet dining.

Raptors have a low rate of reproduction, and the widespread use of the pesticide DDT in the past damaged their eggs. Once DDT or any other pesticide is introduced into the environment, it goes right up the food chain, affecting every life-form, whether it feeds on grass, leaves, insects, fish, birds, or animals. DDT made the shells of the raptors' eggs so thin that when the parent birds sat on them in the nest, their weight crushed the eggshells, killing the embryo chicks.

These factors, combined with extermination by hunters, brought raptors to the brink of extinction in this country. Even the bald eagle, our national bird, was nearly wiped out. Recently, scientists have begun to point out the important role these birds play in the ecosystem, keeping the populations of mice, rats, squirrels, frogs, and some insects under control. So now they are protected by law, and people who kill raptors can be arrested and fined. Also, professional research and rehabilitation work to help raptors increase is under way in a number of places.

When you see a bird of prey capture and carry off a struggling, crying bird or small animal, it's natural to feel sorry for the victim. But we have to remember that our companion animals—our dogs and cats—would do the same if we didn't feed them. Raptors, like everyone else, must eat to survive.

Because of their involvement with saving life, many of the staff at Lifeline for Wildlife see all animals in a different light and have begun to question attitudes they grew up with. Following Betsy's example, many have become vegetarian.

"It's known that human beings can live perfectly well without eating meat, and in fact none of us at Lifeline has suffered any loss of health whatsoever," she says.

Hunters often remind their critics of the inconsistency they see in people who denounce them for killing wildlife but who themselves eat animals and birds that have been raised in captivity and killed in slaughterhouses. They have a point.

Some people excuse hunting on the grounds that it's natural for man to be a predator. It's true that primitive man was both a gatherer of vegetation and a hunter, taking from his environment what he needed for survival. Primitive people killed not just for food—they used every part of an animal for clothing, blankets, tools, weapons. They had to, for there were no substitute materials for these necessities as there are today.

Hunters usually eat what they kill, for game is considered a delicacy. Sometimes hunting provides a welcome addition to the tables of low-income families. But the overwhelming attraction of hunting is for recreation. Hunting gear and equipment support a multibillion-dollar industry. Hunters consider themselves nature lovers; they like to be out in the fresh air with their friends, and they regard hunting as a true contest between themselves and the creatures they consider game.

"No one can honestly view hunting as a fair contest between a human hunter and an animal or bird—a gun or a powerful bow and arrow weighs the odds heavily in favor of the hunter," Marc Payne points out. "And even guns and bows and arrows aren't enough for hunters—they use telescopic gunsights, decoys, blinds, dogs, horses, snowmobiles, and helicopters, among other aids, to increase their advantage. And despite the pleasure of being outdoors and enjoying nature, the object of all this is to kill.''

A popular argument in favor of hunting maintains that certain animals (game animals) must be killed by hunting every year because they have overpopulated, exceeding their habitat, and vast numbers would starve to death. This justification presents hunting as a necessary humanitarian practice.

In fact, however, hunting keeps a game species continually in a speeded-up phase of the animals' reproductive cycle. When animals are killed and removed from a particular habitat, more food obviously becomes available to the remaining animals, and more food stimulates reproduction. So, more animals are born, again putting pressure on the food supply of the land and creating a so-called surplus of animals. Hunting itself helps bring about more animals than a habitat can support.

Wild animal populations will regulate themselves if left alone. Their numbers in a particular habitat may increase over a period of a few years, but then a harsh winter, overcrowding, or reduced food supply will bring about a natural die-off of weaker individuals. Natural adverse conditions also cause a lowered birthrate, and fewer young are born. So in the long run, a wild animal population in a given habitat will be limited by nature to what that habitat can support.

When natural causes weed out the weaker creatures in a particular population, the group as a whole is strengthened. Those that survive are the more fit, and they pass on their superior traits to their offspring.

Hunters, however, kill the best specimens of a game species —the deer with the most impressive antlers, for example. Hunting leaves the weaker members of an animal population to reproduce. In one heavily hunted area of New York State, hunters are now said to be complaining that the deer are small and puny— a condition their ''sport'' has brought about.

Also, hunters remove the animals they kill from the scene.

When a wild animal or bird dies normally in the wild, its carcass is recycled, serving as food for other animals and birds. In nature, nothing is wasted.

Some environmentalists object to hunting not so much for the killing itself as for the assumption, which hunters reflect, that the natural world exists only to be exploited by human beings in any way they choose. Hunters show no respect for the so-called lower forms of life; they fail to understand that all wild species play a role in the balance of life within an ecosystem and are essential to the health of our earth.

Marc Payne sees Lifeline as very much a part of a larger movement. "There's a need for wildlife rehabilitation centers, because they teach people to respect natural forms of life," he says. "Just as hunting, in my opinion, brings out the worst in human beings, wildlife rehabilitation brings out the best—both in those of us who do the work and in the people who bring the wild creatures to us."

7 Interns Speak

It is now an afternoon in late summer at the Ellenville Center, and the many large outdoor compounds and tall cages are filled with wild animals and birds. The structures—made of wood frame and heavy metal fencing—are spaced about the property, some fairly close together, some set off by themselves. They range from small compounds for just a single animal or two to large enclosures that can hold a whole colony of social animals, such as raccoons, squirrels, or skunks. Vertical cages are tall enough to permit birds to fly about.

All the structures are filled with trees, bushes, logs, and brush of the various kinds that the creatures would find in the wild and include wooden boxes to serve as shelters when needed.

The farmhouse itself, set a little way back from the road, is a simple wood-frame building with a porch across the front. In back of it rises a wooded hillside. Farmland, fields, and woods stretch on both sides, with no nearby houses.

A group of young raccoons are milling around in their large compound, climbing up the tree trunks, crawling in and out of the hollow logs, clambering and swinging on the tire that has been hung there for them to play with. Many other raccoons, however, are curled up asleep in the logs, boxes, and other hiding places. Because raccoons are normally nocturnal—active mostly at night—Marc Payne has begun to feed them in the evening instead of in the daytime. They are beginning to shift their schedule accordingly.

The young skunks can hardly be seen at all—they are snugly sound asleep, piles of them together. They are also nocturnal animals and have already begun to sleep throughout most of the day.

Several squirrels, however, are romping furiously in a game of chase. One of them had been a pet, but at Lifeline he has been kept with the other squirrels and not handled, and he has reverted to wildness. When release time comes for his companions, he can safely go with them.

Up on the hillside in back of the farmhouse, secluded from the other cages, a small enclosure is set in the tall grass, with a box inside for the sole occupant to hide in. A little gray fox peers warily out. She was brought to the Lifeline hospital as a very sick infant—Dr. Lerman thought she might have been poisoned by pesticide. But she recovered, and though she was quite tame when she was transferred to Ellenville, she is gradually acquiring her instinctual fear of human beings. She will be released soon.

An opossum who lost a foot in a leghold trap is nearly healed and is beginning to get about fairly comfortably. A mourning dove who was shot in the eye with a BB gun is fully recovered now, though permanently blind in that eye. Both creatures will bear the scars of human cruelty for the rest of their lives.

A young blue jay and an adolescent robin still gape for food whenever anyone comes near their cage, even though they are able to feed themselves. They were fed all summer not only by the student interns but by a male robin who was caged with them and who spent much of his time poking dog food and mealworms into the squalling youngsters' seemingly bottomless gullets. But the adult bird was released recently, and the youngsters are almost ready to go.

Since some of the birds that are released return to look for

Opposite, from top to bottom: *This raccoon thinks it's fun to climb up to the top of the hanging tire in one of the cages at Ellenville. In fact, it's fun to play inside it too. Hide-and-seek?*

meals during the first days or weeks of their freedom, food is always left outside their cages. Quickly, however, they get used to finding their own food and don't come around looking for handouts any longer.

A baby screech owl is eagerly munching on a dead mouse. A two-year-old sea gull that was once somebody's pet is biding his time, waiting to be transferred to a shore-bird rehabilitator on the coast. A crow cocks his head at everything that is going on.

"Crows are smart," says Marc, tossing this one a handful of corn. "They love eggs. I've seen a crow follow a duck around waiting for her to lay an egg. He'd grab the egg and carefully break it open on a rock, because he apparently knew that if he broke it on the ground, some of the contents would soak into the earth before he could eat it up."

Passing among the cages, hard at work, are several interns— high school and college students who live, dormitory-style, at the farmhouse, sharing the housekeeping. After being interviewed closely by Betsy, they signed on to learn about and help take care of the wildlife. Some have come for a week or two; some have been here all summer.

While a great deal of their work consists of feeding the wild-lings and cleaning their compounds, the students also participate, under supervision, in nearly every phase of wildlife rescue, medical care, rehabilitation, and release. Academic credit for their work is arranged with their schools if they wish it.

This afternoon, some of the interns are gathering grasses and leaves for their patients to eat; others are cleaning out the cages. One intern is giving fresh water to seven dogs who are tethered in the shade on the lawn. These dogs are paying guests under the Canine and Feline Vacations program. The interns take them for long walks, play with them several times a day, and bring them into the farmhouse at night. But during much of the day, the dogs lounge around outdoors, watching the activity or sleeping. Feline guests live in the farmhouse.

It's a hot day, and the young people mop their brows and complain as they go about their jobs. But the thought that there

Cages must be cleaned out daily. Below: Gathering special grasses for a vegetarian wildling on the hill in back of the farmhouse and cages

Interns at the swimming hole after a day's work. A beautiful setting to take a shower in.

will be a trip to the swimming hole at the end of the afternoon cheers them up.

Jim Laura, a high school senior, comes down the hillside in back of the farmhouse with his arms full of sumac vines. He dumps the load on the ground and rubs his head.

"What's the matter?" asks Marc, who is repairing a fence on one of the compounds.

"While I was picking sumac for my fawn, the branch of a tree fell and hit me on the head," replies Jim. "I saw stars! But I'm okay, it was just a bump." The fawn he is in charge of is a little over four months old, and Jim is trying to wean him from the bottle. Naturally, no animal can be released until it can feed itself.

"Here you are, kid. I hope it's worth the trouble I went to, to get this for you," Jim remarks as he opens the gate to the animal's compound and goes in. "Ow!" he yells. The half-grown buck has kicked him smartly in the shins.

"This is just too much," Jim says in disgust, throwing down the sumac and stamping out of the enclosure.

Later, Jim gripes to his fellow interns. "First my head, then my shins," he grumbles. The others laugh sympathetically. They have all had their swim and are now sitting around the big table in the farmhouse, finishing dinner. They lounge in their chairs, tired from the day's work but relaxed from the cool swim.

"Listen, I'll never forget one of my first experiences in wildlife rehabilitation," says Ria. "It was not long after I'd joined Lifeline as a volunteer. I came to work at the hospital one morning, and

Hanging out with the dogs after dinner

Judy Lapine handed me the telephone with a funny little smile. 'I believe this call's for you,' she said.

"It was a woman reporting that there was a skunk on her property with a glass jar over its head. The animal apparently had been raiding the garbage can, gone after some food left in the bottom of a jar, and gotten its head stuck. Since I was the new girl at Lifeline, it was my job to go to the woman's house and free the skunk or bring it back to the hospital if necessary."

The interns look at Ria with knowing sympathy. While baby skunks can be handled easily and rarely spray, an adult wild skunk must be treated with extreme caution.

"Sure enough, there was the poor skunk running around in circles, struggling frantically to get its head out of that jar," Ria continues. "It's a wonder it hadn't suffocated. I grabbed it with a blanket, held on to it, and pulled hard on the jar. I got it off. The skunk seemed okay, not hurt at all, so I just let it go.

"Did I get sprayed? I sure did. That skunk really let me have it. I had to shower for what seemed like hours, wash my hair, soak my clothes—even bury some of them. I learned one important lesson in wildlife rescue: You can save an animal's life, and not only does it not thank you, but it may even try to fight you."

"But on the other hand, Ria, there were those three starlings that you raised last spring," comments blonde Kathy Carey, a high school sophomore wearing a pink T-shirt that says SAVE THE WHALES across the front. "After you released them, they stayed around for weeks, and every time you appeared outdoors, they flew down and followed you everywhere you went."

"That's true," agrees Ria. "But they finally went their own way, just as they should."

"Speaking of skunks," says Kathy, "I was amazed to discover how appealing and gentle they can be. They have a bad reputation, but when you get to know them, you can see they're really nice animals. They just defend themselves in the only way they know how when they think they have to. And even though they all look so much alike, each skunk is different from the others, with its own personality."

She pauses, leaning back in her chair. "Working closely with animals certainly teaches you patience and self-control. This will help me all my life." Kathy plans to become a veterinarian. "To me, the down side of wildlife rehabilitation is not so much the hard work and long hours, but not being able to cuddle the baby animals. I know it wouldn't be good for them, but sometimes it's tempting."

"I like feeding the baby birds," Donna Wenz puts in. Seventeen-year-old Donna plans to major in music in college but nevertheless finds caring for the wild creatures a fulfilling experience. "They huddle together with their beaks open, crying and gaping for food so desperately. I get such a kick out of stuffing food with my fingers into their tiny beaks just as if I were their mother." She smiles at the thought. "Wildlife rehabilitation organizations take care of the animals that nobody else helps. I like that."

"I was only kidding about expecting gratitude from my fawn," says Jim, stirring his coffee. "I like him, he's interesting to watch. A lot of the animals show intelligence, even humor—they're more fun than television. But actually, what I like best about wildlife rehabilitation is seeing the animals released, watching them take off without looking back. That's the reward in this work, knowing they're free. The releases make all the cage cleaning and kicks in the shins worthwhile."

The summer is drawing to a close, and soon the interns will be going back to school. They are in a reflective mood, realizing that they will be leaving one another and the wild creatures they have cared so much about. To them, the close contact they've had with the animals and birds is a never-ending source of wonder.

"I never knew much about even the common wildlife before this summer," admits fifteen-year-old Andrew Kamchi.

"You don't have to apologize." Ria smiles. "Most of us are taking care of animals and birds we've never had any contact with before. One day when I was cleaning cages at the hospital, I came to a swan that had just been brought in. There was something wrong with its legs, and it was just sitting there quietly. But as I opened the cage, it stood up and spread its wings, and it was enormous! I'd seen swans, of course, but had never real-

ized how *big* they are until I met this one eye-to-eye. I just cleaned around that bird *very* carefully."

"I hope people realize before it's too late that we need wild animals in the world," Andrew goes on. "The animals have a right to exist. My uncle took me hunting once when I was a child. The eyes of the animals that he shot seemed to look right at me. Working in wildlife rehabilitation has helped me deal with my feelings about that." He hesitates a minute, then adds quietly, "One day, one of the raccoons reached up and took my hand in his. I'll never forget that."

The interns nod. They have all had similar experiences.

"I know what you mean," says Ria. Black-haired Ria, sensible and competent, had been an art major in college, but is taking time out because she enjoys her work with animals so much. "People have always taken advantage of animals," she continues. "I feel that I should do my part to make it up to them.

"One time a man who had found a helpless baby opossum called up and wanted to know if he could bring it to Lifeline. He told me it seemed funny to him to be trying to help this wild animal, because he liked to hunt. The irony of it struck him. We talked a bit when he brought in the opossum. When he left, he said, 'I guess I have some thinking to do.'

"After I talked to that hunter, I came to believe that wildlife rehabilitators can open up avenues of discourse between people on the rights of animals and the value of their lives."

"Some people you just can't talk to," observes Andrew. "I once heard a guy say that deer and raccoons should be harvested, as if they were oranges and beans. He couldn't see the difference."

The young men and women are silent for a while, listening to the evening murmurings and chatterings of the birds and animals outside and watching the twilight gather beyond the windows of the farmhouse. They sit stroking the dogs who lie at their feet or sit on their laps.

Opposite, from top to bottom: *A good place to release a woodchuck.* *"What are you waiting for—you're free!"*

Then Ria, looking pensive, says, "It really bothered me at first whenever an animal or bird died—in fact, it still does, to some extent.

"Were any of you here when we had Cubby? He was that raccoon who had been a pet for *six years.* He was such a pitiful case. The couple who had owned him got divorced, and neither of them wanted Cubby, so they gave him to Lifeline. He was so bewildered. He could never have been released—his owners had had him neutered, and he was too tame. He wouldn't have become sufficiently afraid of people, and he wasn't aggressive enough to defend himself from other animals if he had to. Cubby was with us for a while, and then he died suddenly of unknown causes. He never did have a life of his own in the wild.

"What makes the work most fulfilling for us is what you said, Jim—releasing the animals when they can make it in their natural habitats, knowing they're free. Cubby never had a chance."

A wild bird is strong enough now to be on its own. "Hold it just so."

The moment rehabilitators work toward

Just then, Marc comes in from feeding the raccoons. "Who wants to go to Fahnstock State Park tomorrow to release some animals?" he asks.

Everybody says, "I do!"

Lifeline for Wildlife will soon have a unified facility with all rehabilitation activity located in one place. The staff has long been encumbered with the inconvenience of commuting between the offices and veterinary clinic in one town and the Ellenville Center seventy miles away. In 1984, Lifeline purchased a house with thirty-four acres in Stony Point, New York, and made plans to renovate the house; construct a large building to hold an office, interns' quarters, veterinary clinic, and indoor cages; and build many outdoor cages in the woodland setting.

Betsy Lewis and Mark Lerman explore the new property on which the future Lifeline for Wildlife rehabilitation center will be built.

8 Other Rehabilitators

In Lynnwood, Washington, near Seattle, a wildlife rehabilitation center called HOWL—Help Our Wildlife—opened in 1981 as part of an animal shelter organization, the Progressive Animal Welfare Society (PAWS). In a recent year, HOWL received some thirteen hundred wild animals and birds ranging from woodpeckers and songbirds to barred owls and nighthawks, from squirrels and raccoons to black bears and coyotes. Approximately 50 percent lived to be released.

"The creatures brought to HOWL are usually suffering from injuries caused by people—they have been shot, trapped, poisoned, or hit by cars," says Curtiss Clumpner, who, with Debbie Johnson, is in charge of HOWL. "Also, as with wildlife everywhere, often their habitat has been taken away from them, forcing them into residential areas where they are unwelcome. Sometimes we get birds that have flown into power lines. And many wildlings of all kinds are made homeless by logging."

To its present facility, HOWL will soon add eighteen acres of woodland on which will be built outdoor, naturalistic cages similar to those at Lifeline's Ellenville Center.

"Rehabilitation in Washington is a rapidly expanding craft," says Clumpner. "Today there are approximately eighty people here holding permits. We have our own Washington State Wildlife Rehabilitation Council and meet regularly to discuss our work and to read papers on various topics relating to it."

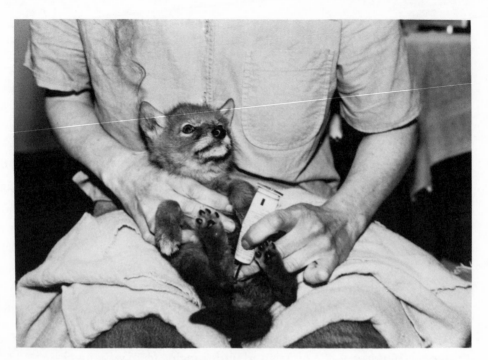

At Help Our Wildlife (HOWL), an orphaned coyote pup is medicated for a staph infection.

Most humane societies and SPCA's have an arrangement with the wildlife rehabilitators nearest them to accept the wildlings brought to the shelters. However, some shelter organizations, like PAWS, have their own fully staffed rehabilitation centers, such as HOWL. The Monterey County SPCA (California), the Humane Society of Marin (California), and the Wisconsin Humane Society (Milwaukee) are among them. The San Francisco SPCA handles some wildlife in its animal shelter but sends others that need special facilities, such as flight cages or large outdoor compounds, to nearby rehabilitators.

The Monterey County SPCA's wildlife organization, which is named the George Whittell Wildlife Rehabilitation Center, recently found itself caring for a large number of pelicans with slashes across their throats, pouches, or chests. Two local men were convicted on cruelty charges and fined—they had apparently captured the birds and mutilated them, presumably for kicks. Many Californians are in the habit of feeding wild pelicans, so the birds have become quite tame. The fact that it is relatively easy to catch them exposes them to possible harm. The Whittell rehabilitators were able to save and release some of the pelicans, although others died.

Birds and animals of the sea, all over the world, are sometimes attacked by fishermen who accuse them of competing for fish. Japanese fishermen caused international horror and anger a few years ago by driving a herd of dolphins into shallow water and slaughtering them merely for revenge. Marine wildlings are not much safer from human cruelty than those of the land.

The Whittell Wildlife Rehabilitation Center, with its indoor and outdoor cages and veterinary clinic, was designed and built specifically for its function. One of its star features is its raptor flight cage, twenty feet tall and built in an L shape, with perches at each end to give the convalescing birds of prey the opportunity to practice banking in flight. In addition to seabirds and familiar animals of all kinds, Whittell has cared for sea otters, mountain lions, coyotes, and bobcats.

Whittell is collecting data on several different species of wildlings that live in the Monterey area. Many rehabilitators keep careful records and are able to give an accurate picture of the general condition of local wildlife. When a particular species declines or disappears, or when many of its members sicken, something may be going wrong in the environment. Human beings would do well to pay attention for their own safety.

We now know that people cannot afford to use a widespread poison on animal life. Environmentalists as well as animal defenders have long waged a battle against the use of Compound 1080, a poison especially favored by sheep ranchers for use against coyotes. Though the main diet of coyotes is small rodents, in times of famine these handsome doglike beasts do sometimes kill sheep.

However, Compound 1080 kills not only coyotes but also any other animal that eats bait containing it. Then, in turn, it kills any creature that feeds on the poisoned animal's carcass. Because

Compound 1080 is so slow to biodegrade, it is deadly dangerous to the environment and can poison land and water. For many years, it was banned by the U.S. government. But now, under pressure from ranchers, our government is permitting its use again. How many animals and human beings will be harmed by Compound 1080, and how soon, nobody knows.

Some rehabilitators have not set up organizations such as Lifeline for Wildlife but are individuals working alone. The size of a rehabilitation center and the number of people involved are not necessarily an indication of the quality of care given to wildlings.

One person who has been rehabilitating wildlife almost single-handedly for many years is Maxine Guy, who lives in Tubac, Arizona, near the Mexican border. Among the animals she has taken in over the years are bobcat kittens. Some were pets that well-meaning but unknowledgeable people tried to raise; the

Maxine Guy holds an orphaned baby bobcat she raised. Later she taught it to hunt its own food and then released it.

HOPE RYDEN

state wildlife authorities confiscated the bobcats and brought them to Guy.

"I had to teach every one of my bobcats to hunt," she recalls.

Guy has also raised and released deer, quail, great blue herons, and hummingbirds among many other creatures.

"One of my hummingbirds came to me as a fledgling not much more than an inch long," she says. "It had to be fed every fifteen to twenty minutes. The metabolism of hummingbirds is very high —they have to have food continually. So I made a special little carrier for this fledgling and took it everywhere with me and fed it all day long for weeks until it was grown."

Maxine Guy's book, *Care of the Wild Feathered and Furred* (see Additional Information, page 116), is considered one of the best ever written for the layman on this subject.

Wildlife rehabilitators have varied relationships with their state wildlife authorities. Apparently much depends on the personal attitudes of the individuals within a state agency. But in every state, the same people who license wildlife rehabilitators also license hunters and trappers and derive income from the hunting and trapping licenses issued.

These state government departments consider it their duty to provide the best hunting for the "sportsmen" of their state.

One of the functions of wildlife managers is to maintain the deer herds, the quail, and other game at peak supply, because those are the wildlings that hunters like to shoot.

Most wildlife rehabilitators privately are opposed to hunting and trapping, though they may keep quiet about it. Many have been given to understand by their state wildlife authorities that if they were to speak out publicly against these activities, they might lose their rehabilitation permits.

People generally tend to think of our national wildlife refugees as sanctuaries where wild animals and birds are safe from bullets, arrows, and traps. This is not so. Today, hunting, trapping, or both, are permitted in 220 out of 420 wildlife refuges. Each year, hunters win out over the protests of animal defenders and many wildlife scientists, and more refuges are opened to permit killing.

In 1983 and early 1984, as many as 63 refuges were added to the list of places where animals could be hunted, so the trend is definitely in that direction.

Hunting and trapping are allowed in all of our national forests and in most state parks. The only public places remaining where wildlings are left alone are our national parks, except for those in Alaska.

Most Americans not only do not hunt, but several different studies in recent years have indicated that the majority disapprove of sport hunting, by anyone.

Hunters make up only 5 to 6 percent of the total U.S. population, but they are a powerful minority. They support a hugely profitable industry that supplies their gear and equipment. They have an active ally in the National Rifle Association, which works hard to influence lawmakers to oppose any restrictions on gun ownership.

In some states, hunting groups have persuaded lawmakers to introduce laws that would make it illegal for people to interfere with hunting. During the hunting season, animal defenders go into the woods and try to warn the animals by ringing bells, yelling, and making noise. They hope to scare the animals into taking cover. One would think that these animal defenders have as much right to be on public land as the hunters do. But warning the animals is considered to be interfering with the hunters' rights. And so, in some places, a person can be arrested for trying to protect a hunted wild creature or help it escape.

Many people feel that it would be better if public lands such as wildlife refuges, national forests, and state parks could be supported and supervised by neutral agencies that represent the American public as a whole. Hikers and campers, who use and enjoy our wilderness areas, should have a say in what happens to wildlife. People who simply love and respect wild animals and birds should be consulted also. And certainly scientists who oppose hunting as a suitable method by which to deal with temporary overpopulation within an ecosystem should share in the decisions that affect all wildlings.

Though many rehabilitators are self-taught and have learned by doing, reading, and questioning others, professionalism among them is rising. Richard Evans, a veterinarian and president of the National Wildlife Rehabilitators Association, believes that rehabilitators should establish and maintain their own high standards.

"These standards could be used by state agencies as a basis for granting licenses to persons who apply for them," he says.

Evans is director of Treehouse Wildlife Center, in Brighton, Illinois, a facility on nineteen acres of woodland with a complete hospital that includes mammal and bird wards, an intensive-care ward, and an exercise area. Interns live at the hospital.

Some wildlife rehabilitation centers specialize in one type of wild creature. A highly professional facility is the Raptor Research and Rehabilitation Center at the University of Minnesota, where veterinarian Patrick Redig and Professor Gary Duke are conducting important studies on birds of prey. Many owls, hawks, and eagles are brought to them with broken wings, crushed toes, and head injuries, usually caused by cars, power lines, bullets, or traps. This center also receives orphaned raptor chicks, many of whom grow up and are released.

The person who shot this American bald eagle disabled it permanently. Shown here with Dr. Gary Duke, it now lives at the Raptor Research and Rehabilitation Center.

HOPE RYDEN

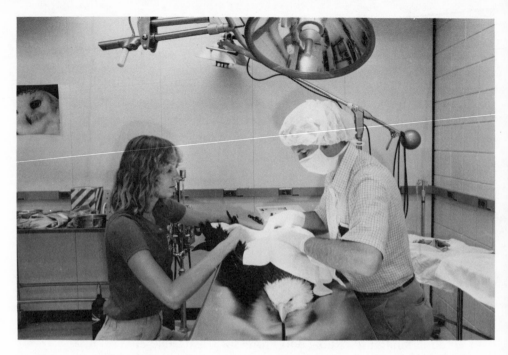

HOPE RYDEN, above and below
Dr. Patrick Redig, assisted by Paula Swenson, performs surgery on a bald eagle. Below: University students prepare to let a convalescing eagle exercise its wings so that eventually it will be strong enough to be set free.

About 40 percent of the center's birds are freed; those that are handicapped but otherwise healthy are kept for breeding.

Student volunteers help in the hospital and also perform an important service for birds that need to exercise their wings during their recovery period. The students fasten bands and lines to the birds' legs, take them outdoors, and fly them aloft like kites. (Whisper, the great horned owl that Marc Payne took care of, went to a raptor rehabilitator who could exercise him in that way.)

On the west coast of Florida, near Tampa, the Suncoast Seabird Sanctuary takes in fifteen to twenty birds a day, the vast majority of whom have been injured by fishing lines and hooks.

"The birds, especially pelicans, become entangled in fishing lines, or they dive for fish that have been caught by people and swallow the hooks," explains Ralph T. Heath, Jr., the founder and director. "Unfortunately, most people, when they accidentally catch a bird with their fishing gear, just cut the line and let the bird fly away, not realizing that the bird is almost certainly doomed. The dangling line becomes entangled in vegetation on the shore, trapping the bird, who slowly dies of hunger and thirst. Or, if a bird has a fishhook embedded in its flesh, it usually dies from infection."

Heath has published two free brochures: *Help for Hooked Birds* and *The Care and Feeding of Orphan Song and Garden Birds* (see Additional Information, page 117).

The Suncoast Seabird Sanctuary has nine full-time employees and many volunteers, some of whom are college students who receive academic credit for their work. It is open to visitors daily, year-round, from 9 A.M. until dark.

A wildlife rehabilitation organization that specializes in a different kind of creature is the California Marine Mammal Center, near San Francisco. At any given time, the staff here is caring for perhaps twenty seals and sea lions that have beached themselves on the California coast in some kind of trouble. Orphaned, sick, or injured, they are gathered up by staff members and volunteers who may have driven several hundred miles to get them. SPCA's

ERNIE SIMMONS

*A young brown pelican injured by a fishhook is fortunate to have
been brought to Suncoast Seabird Sanctuary, where it will be treated
and cared for by Ralph and Beatrice Heath until it is well.*

A couple of patients at the California Marine Mammal Center are given their pills and then rewarded with tasty fish.

and Fish and Game Departments all along the coast notify the Marine Mammal Center whenever a pinniped, as these creatures are called scientifically, is spotted on a beach and needs help.

The seals and sea lions suffer from propeller and gunshot wounds caused by careless or cruel people, as well as from natural illnesses and injuries. About 65 percent of those treated at the Marine Mammal Center live to be put back in the ocean.

Wildlings of the fields and forests, swamps and shores, plains and mountains are struggling to survive against formidable dangers and tough enemies. Rehabilitators may be, in the most direct way, the best friends the wild animals and birds have. Like the staff at Lifeline for Wildlife, these people believe wild creatures have a right to their lives and to a share of the earth. They feel that the planet would be a desolate place without them.

Though rehabilitators affect only a tiny proportion of the total population of most native species, they make it possible for hundreds of thousands of *individuals* to stay alive. And they encourage and honor the compassion of people who bring the injured, sick, and orphaned to them for help. They set an example for us.

Wildlife rehabilitation plays an important part in the movement to teach respect for our earth and its wonderful variety of living creatures.

9 What You Can Do To Help Wildlife

There are many things a caring person can do to help wild animals and birds, both directly and indirectly. Direct help means the hands-on care you give when you find an injured, sick, or orphaned wild creature. Suggestions on this subject will be detailed here.

But first, giving indirect help to wildlings is something you can do every day, all of your life. It means embracing a point of view, a philosophy, that millions of compassionate people around the world have held for hundreds of years. The idea that wildlife is entitled to a share of the planet is not new, though human behavior throughout history has reflected the opposite attitude. People have often acted as if the earth and all other life-forms are theirs alone to use in any way they choose.

One scientist in charge of a program for helping endangered birds to survive was asked recently by a reporter why people should bother to preserve endangered species. The scientist reacted as if the reporter had asked him why people should bother to breathe! It seemed to him so obvious that all life-forms are interconnected and dependent on each other for survival that he had taken it for granted that everybody knew it.

People who are sympathetic toward wildlife will often be told by others, in a condescending way, that their concern is nothing more than the "Bambi syndrome." This accusation refers to the sentimental view of wildlife depicted in the animated cartoon movie *Bambi* and in the book on which the movie was based.

However, caring what happens to wildlife is a matter of justice, not of sentimentality. You don't have to get teary-eyed over the plight of a fawn to believe that the animal is entitled to its life.

One good way to help wildlife is to join the many people who believe that other life-forms also have rights and that it is in their own best interests as human beings to treat them with compassion and respect.

Therefore, don't hunt wild creatures, don't trap them, don't eat them, and don't wear their skins.

Don't fall for the argument that since the animals whose pelts went into a fur coat were already dead when the coat was made, there is nothing wrong with wearing the coat. True, you can't help the individual animals who were killed to make up a particular coat. But people who buy furs keep furriers in business, who in turn encourage the trappers to go out and kill more and more animals. Wearing furs tells the world, in effect, that killing animals for their skins is an acceptable thing to do.

While the fur coat industry is prosperous, by the way, trappers generally are not. However, trapping is virtually never their only means of earning a living. It is an occupation of choice.

Don't be misled by the fact that many furs come not from trapped wild animals but from captive animals raised on so-called ranches. These ranches are inhumane places where normally wild fur-bearing animals are raised in tight cages, often in foul-smelling buildings, until they are slaughtered and skinned.

Inform yourself about the true nature of wild creatures and their needs. There are many interesting and accurate books about them in your library and bookstore. (For a listing of some, see pages 116–117.) Informative nature magazines, as well as TV programs on nature, especially those on the National Educational Television network, can teach you a great deal as well as entertain you. (If you are familiar with the magazine *Ranger Rick,* by the way, be aware that it is published by the National Wildlife Federation, an organization that favors sport hunting.)

The more you know about wildlings, the more you'll be able

to enjoy and appreciate them—and you'll also be better able to understand public issues regarding them.

For instance, is the government's decision to allow the use of the poisonous Compound 1080 to kill wild animals a wise move? Or is it based on pressure from ranchers who choose to ignore the long-term environmental dangers of 1080 in exchange for their own short-term benefit? When the government wants to round up and remove wild horses from their refuge because, according to its nose count, the herds need "thinning," is this a real necessity? Or is the proposed roundup motivated by someone's economic interest?

When the government decides to allow hunting in a state park, is there truly an overpopulation of certain game animals? If so, has it been created artificially? If left alone, would the animal population eventually self-regulate according to the available food supply? And will hunting in a state park benefit all the people who enjoy the park—or just the hunters and the state agency that receives income from the hunting licenses?

Are there ways for state wildlife departments to get their operating funds other than through hunting, trapping, and fishing licenses? Could money for wildlife protection be raised in other ways, such as a bottle tax or a tax on camping equipment?

These are the kinds of important issues that citizens must deal with continually. To understand them requires a good deal of solid information and a sophisticated viewpoint. You can educate yourself by reading and thinking about whose interests might really lie behind each particular issue. If you learn the facts and find out whose opinions you can trust and whose to question, you can participate wisely in making decisions that affect the welfare of wildlife. You'll be able to vote soon. And if you write your legislators on important matters from an informed position, your opinions will be taken seriously.

When reading about wildlife, it's a good idea to take into consideration the point of view the authors represent. For example, a group of western fish and game agencies, under the guise of teaching environmental education, has published a set of manuals called *Project Wild* for classroom use by elementary and secondary school teachers. The sponsors are attempting to place these books in public and private schools throughout the United States.

The books urge teachers to encourage children to learn a great deal about wildlife and environmental issues—and to regard hunting as an acceptable activity. Though *Project Wild* appears to present a balanced view, when you read the manuals thoughtfully, you can see that they are one-sided and reflect only the views of wildlife managers and hunters. The text does mention briefly that objections to hunting and trapping do exist, but it never explains the sound scientific or ethical reasons for this opposition. Instead, arguments in favor are carefully pressed home.

Two romantic stories glorifying the joy of hunting are included in the books—yet there are no stories of young people who don't wish to kill wildlife. Nowhere is there any mention whatsoever of the suffering that hunting and trapping cause. The violent and painful deaths of hunted and trapped wildlings are pointedly omitted from any of the classroom exercises, discussions, or assignments suggested.

Though teachers are advised to allow students to hear all viewpoints on wildlife issues, students are then instructed on ways to "neutralize" other children who do not agree with them. So, if your class were following a *Project Wild* curriculum, your classmates might attempt to silence you if you voiced an opinion that hunting is cruel and unnecessary. So-called radical views, even if they happen to be the views of most Americans, are not to be tolerated, according to *Project Wild*.

In these books, wild animals and birds are called a renewable resource, like trees, part of the natural world that is presumed to exist only for human use. In *Project Wild,* the right of wild creatures to exist is not seen as an issue worth debating.

Another very important way to help wildlings, even when you don't see them, is to respect their habitats. Never do anything in the woods, fields, desert, mountains, shores, or water that could cause them harm.

This means obeying all the rules about campfires. It means not driving off-the-road vehicles where wildlife dwellings would be disturbed. It means not littering. One particular danger to wildlife on land and sea is the plastic holder for a six-pack of soft drinks or beer. Birds and animals become entangled in these empty holders that people thoughtlessly discard.

Dogs and cats are responsible for harm to wildlife living near human habitations. If pets were confined—dogs kept in fenced yards and walked on leashes, cats kept indoors and closely supervised when outdoors—thousands of wild creatures, especially babies, would be spared injury or death.

As for direct ways to help individual wild creatures when you encounter them, the first thing to determine is whether they truly need assistance. It's usually easy enough to see if they are injured or sick by the way they look and act. But judging whether or not they are orphaned is often difficult. It is not uncommon for well-meaning people to "rescue" an infant that they assume is orphaned simply because they don't see the mother around.

Be extremely cautious about handling any wild creature. Naturally, it will be afraid of you and, especially if it is in pain, it may try to bite you. Get an experienced person to help you or, better yet, if possible get the people at a wildlife rehabilitation center to come and capture any wildling that seems difficult or dangerous.

If an animal seems sick, weak, or disoriented, *don't touch it.* It might have distemper or rabies. Bats especially, by the way, are known to be carriers of rabies. Use a shovel, gently, to get the creature into a carton or empty garbage can and take it to a wildlife rehabilitation center. If you don't know of one in your area, ask your state fish and game agency for help. Don't just leave an animal that may be rabid—not only is it suffering but it's dangerous to other animals as well as people.

If you do take a wild creature home temporarily, keep it in a warm, quiet place. Don't call in your friends and neighbors to see it—this might cause it to die from fright or stress.

If it is wounded, find a veterinarian or an experienced person who will give it first aid, especially if you can't get it to a rehabilitator for several hours.

Some wildlings can be offered food, cautiously. (See suggestions for direct ways to help, starting below.)

Now is the time to put out of your head any thoughts of keeping the wildling as a pet. Remember those animals and birds that were turned in to Lifeline for Wildlife and to other rehabilitators after their owners discovered that they didn't make good pets. Eventually you would regret keeping the creature and, most important, you'd be depriving it of a normal life.

And remember that it is illegal to keep a wild creature without a permit. If the authorities discover that you have one, you will be fined and the wildling will be taken away from you.

By now, you know that the very best way you can help a wild animal or bird that's in trouble is to turn it over to a wildlife rehabilitator. How do you locate one?

Your local humane society, SPCA, or other animal welfare organization may be able to refer you to one. The animal shelter people may even offer to take the creature from you and get it to a rehabilitation center.

A zoo or nature center may be able to direct you to a rehabilitator also.

An office of the Audubon Society, Sierra Club, or other environmental group may know of a nearby rehabilitation center.

Private veterinarians may know about wildlife rehabilitators. Some will also give first aid or emergency treatment to a seriously wounded wild animal.

Your local game warden or someone at the nearest office of the state fish and game department (whatever it's called in your state) may refer you to a wildlife rehabilitation center. Since these departments license rehabilitators, they are in a position to have that information.

Here are suggestions for direct ways to help specific wildlings:

Baby bird   If it has simply fallen out of the nest, gently put it back. You may have heard that a mother bird will reject her young if they have been handled by people. This is not true.

If you find a baby bird on the ground that is trying to learn to fly, just leave the scene and, if you can, keep dogs and cats away for a day or two.

If you find a helpless baby bird on the ground with no nest and no mother bird in sight, that one probably needs your help. Put the little creature in a plastic berry basket or small box lined with facial tissue. Don't use dirt or leaves to line this "nest"—such stuff can contain harmful parasites and bacteria.

Give it first aid until you can get it to a rehabilitation center. Put the basket or box in a small carton, cover the carton, and put it on a heating pad (turned on low) or a hot-water bottle (warm, wrapped in a towel). Don't wrap the bird in anything and don't put it in the sun—it will overheat.

As soon as the bird is warm, offer it warm milk with a bit of sugar in it through a plastic medicine dropper. If necessary, open its beak very gently. Don't squirt the milk down its throat, but give it one drop at a time. Make sure it swallows each drop before you give it another. Being warm and having some liquid nourishment should help keep the bird alive until you can get it to a professional.

Injured bird   Capture it as gently as you can and put it in a carton, preferably with screening or wire mesh on the bottom for it to cling to. If it seems to have a broken wing or leg, don't move the injured part. Immobilize the bird so as to prevent further injury. One way to do this is to make a poncho from a clean rag. Cut a small hole in the middle and slip the bird's head through the hole. Draw the rag over the bird's body and fasten the ends of the rag together with a safety pin.

Keep the bird warm and quiet until you take it to a rehabilitator.

Trapped bird   Don't simply free it from the trap and allow it to fly away—chances are that because the blood supply has been cut off from the place where the trap held it, gangrene has set in. Gangrene doesn't always show up right away, but eventually it will cause the bird to suffer for a long time and then die. Therefore, medical treatment is essential. Capture the bird before you open the trap, hold on to it, and get it to a rehabilitator.

Bird entangled in fishing line   Never just cut the line and let the bird fly off. It is absolutely essential to disentangle the bird totally from the line before letting it go, or the dangling line may become caught in vegetation, trapping the bird. If you are unable to untangle it, take it to a professional rehabilitator. This is a good idea anyway, because the rehabilitator will also check the bird and treat any injuries before setting it free.

Bird with fishhook in its flesh   Again, don't just cut the fishing line and free the bird with the hook still in it—the bird will almost surely die from infection. Medical treatment is required, so take the bird to a rehabilitation center.

Baby rabbit   Normally, a mother rabbit comes to her nest only once or twice a day to nurse her babies, so if you find a nest of infant rabbits alone, it doesn't mean that their mother has deserted them. If they appear healthy, remember where they are and come back the next day to check on them. If they still seem okay, you can assume the mother is alive and taking care of them. Try to see that they are left alone by nosy people and pets.

If you know or have very good reason to believe that the baby rabbits truly are orphaned, put them gently in a box, cover it, keep them quiet and warm, and take them to a rehabilitation center as soon as possible. Baby rabbits are fragile, so don't be disappointed if some don't live to reach the rehabilitator.

If you find a baby rabbit out of the nest, watch to see if it is eating. If so, that means it is old enough to take care of itself, so leave it alone.

Infant raccoon, squirrel, skunk, or other very small mammal   If you are certain it is orphaned and too young to feed itself, wrap it in something warm, especially if it is hairless and its eyes are still shut. If there are several animals together, put them in a small box with soft rags and keep them warm. Cover the box. You can put the box on a heating pad, but turn it on low and check to be sure it's not overheating. Get the animals to a rehabilitation center as fast as possible.

Baby deer   Unless a fawn is injured or you have proof that its mother is dead, leave it alone. Many infant fawns are rescued by mistake. Like a mother rabbit, a doe comes only once or twice in twenty-four hours to nurse her baby, often only at night. Fawns are programmed to remain where their mother leaves them. If disturbed, they will drop to the ground and not move.

A fawn who is wandering on a road, hurt, trapped, or harassed by dogs or people definitely should be rescued. Fawns are easily stressed, so wrap it or put it in a covered cage and keep it as quiet as possible. Take it to a rehabilitation center or telephone the center and ask someone to come and pick it up. Meanwhile, if it is willing to nurse from a baby bottle or pet nursing bottle, offer it some warm milk with some baby cereal mixed in to give it a little nourishment.

Trapped animal   The same advice goes for trapped animals as for trapped birds—don't simply free them, because the trap will undoubtedly have shut off the blood supply enough to cause gangrene, which will ultimately kill the animal by degrees. Be extremely careful in freeing the animal, because it may be crazed by fear, exposure, pain, hunger, and thirst and may try to bite you. You need to immobilize it by covering it with a blanket or coat while someone else opens the trap. Restrain it so it can't hurt you or escape, and get it to a rehabilitation center as soon as possible.

You might offer it some water and food first. As for what to feed it, here's where a knowledge of wildlife comes in handy. If you don't know what the animal eats, ask someone who is well-informed about the particular species of creature you have found.

Opossums   If you find a dead female opossum, look for in-fants on her body or in her pouch. If you find any, take the mother's body to a rehabilitation center. The babies will be better off staying in her pouch than in a box by themselves on the way to the rehabilitator.

Baby opossums normally stay in the pouch until they are ready to forage on their own. If you find one alone that's obviously too young to feed itself, it's in trouble, so put it in a box, keep it warm and quiet, and take it to a rehabilitator.

If you can give the right kind of first aid and immediate supportive care to an orphaned or injured wildling, you may make the difference between its life and death. Then, when you deliver it to a rehabilitator, you know you have done your best for it.

Additional Information

BOOKS

Care of the Wild Feathered and Furred: Treating and Feeding Injured Birds and Animals by Mae Hickman and Maxine Guy. Available for $10.95 (postage included) from Maxine Guy, Box 1243, Tubac, Arizona 85640.

Wild Orphan Babies: Caring for Them and Setting Them Free by William J. Weber, D.V.M. New York: Holt, Rinehart & Winston, 1975.

The Suncoast Seabird Sanctuary by Frances E. Wood and Ralph T. Heath, Jr. Available for $4.50 (postage included) from the Suncoast Seabird Sanctuary, 18328 Gulf Boulevard, Indian Shores, Florida 33535.

Second Chance: The Affectionate Story of One Family's Efforts to Heal Sick Birds and Marine Mammals and Return Them to the Wild by Alan Bryant. New York: St. Martin's Press, 1981.

Pearson, a Harbor Seal Pup. The rehabilitation of a stranded California seal. By Susan Meyers. New York: E. P. Dutton, 1980.

Unexpected Treasure. Tender story of a wildlife refuge. By Hope Sawyer Buyukmihci with Hans Fantel. Available for $7 (postage included) from Unexpected Wildlife Refuge, Newfield, New Jersey 08344.

Facts About Furs. Thorough and incontrovertible indictment of trapping. By Greta Nilsson. Available for $4 (postage included) from Animal Welfare Institute, P.O. Box 3650, Washington, D.C. 20007.

Shoot, Tank, Shoot. A cartoon story in which a he-man sports announcer goes hunting. By Jeff Millar and Bill Hinds. Kansas City: Sheed, Andrews & McMeel, 1977.

Man Kind? Strong exposé of hunting and trapping. By Cleveland Amory. Available for $4.95 (hardcover) or $1.75 (paperback), postage included, from Fund for Animals, 200 West 57th Street, New York, N.Y. 10019.

Secrets of a Wildlife Watcher. Techniques of wildlife observation. By Jim Aronsky. New York: Lothrop, Lee & Shepard, 1983.

Bobcat. Comprehensive story of this little-known North American wild feline. By Hope Ryden. New York: Putnam, 1983.

America's Bald Eagle. Detailed account of this endangered bird's habits. By Hope Ryden. New York: Putnam, 1985.

Bears in the Wild. All about this misunderstood wild mammal. By Ada and Frank Graham. New York: Delacorte, 1981.

Coyote Song. Facts about the wild canid and its plight; a discussion of alternatives to killing. By Ada and Frank Graham. New York: Delacorte, 1978.

Coydog. A boy's friendship with a hybrid wild animal. By Evelyn Wilde Mayerson. New York: Scribner's, 1981.

Exploring the World of Wolves: Wolfman. Biography of the biologist David Mech and his twenty-five-year study of wolves in the wild. By Laurence Pringle. New York: Scribner's, 1983.

BROCHURES

The Care and Feeding of Orphan Song and Garden Birds and *Help for Hooked Birds.* Both free. Send a self-addressed, stamped, business-size envelope to Suncoast Seabird Sanctuary, 18328 Gulf Boulevard, Indian Shores, Florida 33535.

You and the Beaver and *Golden Rules of Conservation.* Available for ten cents each. Send a self-addressed, stamped, business-size envelope to Unexpected Wildlife Refuge, Newfield, New Jersey 08344.

OTHER

Kind News. A newspaper for children who care about animals and want to learn more about them and how to help them. *Kind News I* is for children in grades 1–3; *Kind News II,* for children in grades 4–6. Thirty-five copies of each of four issues (140 newspapers total) of either *Kind News I* or *II* costs $10. Published during the school year by the National Association for the Advancement of Humane Education, P.O. Box 362, East Haddam, Connecticut 06423.

Films for Humane Education. A paperback book that lists, describes, evaluates, and gives all pertinent details on animal films that can be rented or borrowed. Includes many films on wildlife. A valuable aid to librarians, teachers, and group leaders. For details on ordering, write to Argus Archives, 228 East 49th Street, New York, New York 10017.

After the First. A 16mm color film, fourteen minutes long. A boy is given a rifle and taken on his first hunting trip by his father. Later, the boy struggles with the realization of the suffering he has caused. Film rental $20, purchase $300. Videotape rental $15, purchase $145. Available from TeleKETICS Films, Franciscan Communications, 1229 S. Santee Street, Los Angeles, California 90015.

Cedar Run Wildlife Refuge. Open to the public year-round and accessible from New Jersey, New York, Pennsylvania, Delaware, and Maryland. Field trips through the refuge are guided by Elizabeth M. Woodford, an experienced field naturalist and wildlife rehabilitator. Mrs. Woodford also travels throughout the eastern United States to give slide lectures on the wildlife and ecology of the New Jersey Pine Barrens, as well as on wildlife in Africa and South America, seen on the safaris she has led. Cedar Run Wildlife Refuge, R.D. 2, Marlton, New Jersey 08053. 609-983-3329.

Wildlife Rehabilitators

Here, selected at random and grouped according to region, are some wildlife rehabilitation centers to which you can turn to get help for an orphaned or injured wildling. This is by no means a complete list, for there are hundreds of centers, and new ones are opening continually to meet the rising need for them and the growing interest in the field. However, the centers here might be able to rescue a creature that needs help, accept one you have found, give you information and advice, or refer you to a center nearest your home.

Northeast

Vermont Institute
  of Natural Science
Church Hill Road
Woodstock, Vermont 05091

Squam Lake Science Center
Box 146
Holderness, New Hampshire 03245

Dr. Wolf's Animal Center
249 Milton Street
Dedham, Massachusetts 02026

Worcester Science Center
222 Harrington Way
Worcester, Massachusetts 01604

South Shore Wildlife Medical Center
146 A, Justice Cushing Highway
Hingham, Massachusetts 02043

The Mews
P.O. Box 188, Cox Road
Portland, Connecticut 06480

Connecticut Audubon Society
2325 Burr Street
Fairfield, Connecticut 06430

East

Lifeline for Wildlife
R.R. 1, Box 446 A
Blanchard Road
Stony Point, New York 10980

Clearbrook Wildlife Center
Star Route 333, Route 32 N
Cairo, New York 12413

Zoological Society of Buffalo
Delaware Park
Buffalo, New York 14214

Seneca Wildlife Haven
R.R. 2, Box 158
Lodi, New York 14860

Humane Society of Rochester
and Monroe County
99 Victor Road
Fairport, New York 14450

Avian Rehabilitation Center
Box 323
Marmora, New Jersey 08223

North Jersey Raptor Care Center
Box 738 A, Road #2
Andover, New Jersey 07821

PAWS
R.D. 1
Hainesport–Mount Laurel Road
Mount Laurel, New Jersey 08054

Chesapeake Bird Sanctuary
10305 King Richard Place
Upper Marlboro, Maryland 20772

Tri-State Bird Rescue
Delaware Audubon Society
Box 1713
Wilmington, Delaware 19899

Southeast

Wild Bird Rescue League of
Northern Virginia
1930 Hileman Road
Falls Church, Virginia 22043

Hanover Green Veterinary Clinic
1123 Hanover Green Drive
Mechanicsville, Virginia 23111

Volunteer Animal Rescue, Inc.
239 Dominion Drive
Newport News, Virginia 23602

Shenandoah Wildlife
Rehabilitation Center
Route 1, Box 35
Waynesboro, Virginia 22980

Nature Science Center
Museum Drive
Winston-Salem
North Carolina 27105

Felicidades Wildlife Foundation
P.O. Box 490
Waynesville, North Carolina 28786

Carolina Raptor Rehabilitation
and Research Center
Department of Biology
University of North Carolina
Charlotte, North Carolina 28223

North Carolina Museum
of Life Science
433 Murray Avenue
Durham, North Carolina 27704

Suncoast Seabird Sanctuary
18328 Gulf Boulevard
Indian Shores, Florida 33535

Florida Wildlife Sanctuary
2600 Otter Creek Lane
Melbourne, Florida 32935

South

Lichterman Nature Center
5992 Quince Road
Memphis, Tennessee 38119

Wildlife Rescue Service
Box 7633
Birmingham, Alabama 35253

Audubon Wild Bird Rehabilitation
Box 4327
New Orleans, Louisiana 70178

Central

Kalamazoo Nature Center
7000 N. Westnedge Avenue
Kalamazoo, Michigan 49007

James G. Sikarski, D.V.M.
102 B Veterinary Clinic Center
East Lansing, Michigan 48824

Brukner Nature Center
5995 Horseshoe Bend Road
Troy, Ohio 45373

O.A.C.F.
1304 W. Ewing Avenue, Box 2345
South Bend, Indiana 46614

Warrick Wildlife Rehabilitation
8270 Highway 66
Newburgh, Indiana 47630

Treehouse Wildlife Center
Route 1, Box 125 E
Brighton, Illinois 62012

Willowbrook Wildlife Haven
525 S. Park Boulevard
Glen Ellyn, Illinois 60138

Wildlife Rescue Center
147 Grand
Kirkwood, Missouri 63122

Lakeside Nature Center
5600 E. Gregory-Swope Park
Kansas City, Missouri 64132

Wildlife ARC
4151 N. Humboldt
Milwaukee, Wisconsin 53212

Bay Beach Wildlife Sanctuary
100 N. Jefferson Street
Green Bay, Wisconsin 54301

North Woods Wildlife Center
Highway 70 West
Minocqua, Wisconsin 54548

Como Zoo Docent Association
1621 Niles Avenue
St. Paul, Minnesota 55103

West

Wildlife Rescue Team
Route 1, Box 82 A
Walton, Nebraska 68461

Cheyenne Pet Clinic
3720 E. Lincoln Way
Cheyenne, Wyoming 82001

Audubon River Trail Nature
  Center
5200 West 11th Street
Pueblo, Colorado 81003

Colorado Wildlife Rescue
Box 105
Sedalia, Colorado 80135

Southwest

Texas Wildlife Rehabilitation
  Coalition
8829 Croes Drive
Houston, Texas 77055

Wildlife Rescue and Rehabilitation
P.O. Box 34 F F
San Antonio, Texas 78201

Fort Worth Nature Center
Route 10, Box 53
Fort Worth, Texas 76135

Amistad Wildlife Reserve Center
119 Edwards
Del Rio, Texas 78840

Austin Nature Center
401 Deep Eddy
Austin, Texas 78703

Wildlife Rescue of New Mexico
11200 Menaul Boulevard N.E.
Albuquerque, New Mexico
  87112

Maxine Guy
P.O. Box 1243
Tubac, Arizona 85640

West Coast

HOWL
P.O. Box 5574
Lynnwood, Washington 98046

Whidbey Island Wild Animal
Clinic
2416 E. Goodell Road
Langeley, Washington 98260

Audubon Wildlife Rehabilitation
5181 N.W. Cornell Road
Portland, Oregon 97210

Shasta Wildlife Rescue
P.O. Box 359
Shasta, California 96087

Marin Wildlife Center
P.O. Box 957
San Rafael, California 94902

Wildlife Care Association
3615 Auburn Road
Sacramento, California 95821

Lake Tahoe Wildlife Care
P.O. Box 10557
South Lake Tahoe, California
95731

California Marine Mammal Center
Marin Headlands, Fort Cronkhite
Sausalito, California 94968

Fresno Wildlife Rescue
P.O. Box 9032
Fresno, California 93790

Ventana Wilderness Sanctuary
P.O. Box 894
Carmel Valley, California 93924

Monterey County SPCA
P.O. Box 3058
Monterey, California 93942

Bird and Wildlife
Rehabilitation Center
6883 Vista Del Rincon
Ventura, California 93001

Living Desert Reserve
P.O. Box 1775
Palm Desert, California 92260

American Wildlife Rescue Service
1296 Conference Drive
Scotts Valley, California 95066

Hawaii

Hawaiian SPCA
2700 Waialae Avenue
Honolulu, Hawaii 96826

Canada

Salmonier Nature Park
P.O. Box 190, Holyrood
Newfoundland AOA 2RO

Toronto SPCA
11 River Street
Toronto, Ontario M5A 4C2

Essex County SPCA
1375 Provincial Road
Windsor, Ontario N9A 6J3

Erie Wildlife Rescue
Box 252
Amherstburg, Ontario N9U 2Z4

Lower Mainland Wildlife Reserve
4519 Piper Avenue
Burnaby, British Columbia
U5A 3R4

Index

Page numbers in *italics* refer to captions.

amputation, 33, 72
anesthetics, 33–34
animal defenders, 98
animal shelters, 18–19, 94,
   110
  see also wildlife
   rehabilitation centers
ASPCA (American Society for
  the Prevention of Cruelty
  to Animals), 6, 18
Audubon Society, 110
autopsies, 6–7

balance of nature, 27, 77–78
bald eagles, 20, 75, *99, 100*
"Bambi syndrome," 105
bats, 109
bears, 20, 93
birds:
  baby, feeding of, *9,* 11, *12,*
   59, 87, 97, 111
  baby, how to help, 110–111
  caught in traps, 36, 111
  as game, 20, 75
  injured, how to help,
   111–112
  injured by fishhooks, 56, 57,
   101, *102,* 112

birds, *cont'd.*
  raptors, 33, 74–76, 95,
   99–101, *99, 100*
  released into the wild, *iv,*
   13, 18, 29, *73,* 75,
   81–82, 86, *90,* 101
  see also individual species
birthrate, among wild animals,
  77
blue jays, *iv,* 81
bobcats, 95, 96–97, *96*
Bronx Zoo, 39
bumblefoot, 11

cages:
  cleaning of, 2, *83,* 87–89
  naturalistic, 79, 93
  for raptors to fly in, 95
California Marine Mammal
  Center, 101–103, *103*
Canada geese, 45–46
Canine and Feline Vacations,
  24, *28,* 43, 82
*Care and Feeding of Orphan
  Song and Garden Birds,
  The* (Heath), 101
*Care of the Wild Feathered
  and Furred* (Guy), 97

Carey, Kathy, 86–87
catch-poles, 47, *61*
cats, domestic, 21, 36, 109
cats, wild, 20
chimney sweeps, 49, *50*
cleanliness of animals, in the
     wild vs. captivity, 2
Clumpner, Curtiss, 93
come-alongs, 47
Compound 1080, 95–96,
     107
coyotes, 93, *94,* 95
crows, 2, 32–33, *32,* 39, 82
cruelty to animals, 51–53, 81,
     94–95, 103
   by children, 48, 51, 53
Cubby (raccoon), 90
Cupp, Mary Catherine, 64–68,
     65

Dawn, 54–57
DDT, 75
Deacon, Nancy, 31, 32
death of animals, 21, 58, 90
deer:
   hunting of, 20, 77, 89, 97
   released into the wild, 72,
     97
   see also fawns
defecation:
   fear and, 47
   stimulation of, 11, *44*
deformities, among hooved
     animals, 31–32
Department of Environmental
     Conservation, New York
     (DEC), 24–25
distemper, 48, 58, 109
dogs, domestic, 21, 36, 64,
     109
dolphins, 95

domestic animals:
   wild animals vs., 42
   see also pets
doves, 81
ducks, 20
   rescue of, 54–57
Duke, Gary, 99, *99*

eagles, 36, 75, 99
   bald, 20, 75, *99, 100*
ecosystem, 75, 78, 98
eggshells, DDT and, 75
elk, 20
Ellenville, N.Y., Lifeline facility
     at, 13–16, 19–26, 41,
     43–92
   compounds and cages at,
     79, 93
   farmhouse at, *19,* 79
   raccoons at, 13, *14, 15,* 41,
     49, 79, *81*
   see also Lifeline for Wildlife
endangered species, 20, 75,
     105
euthanasia, 33, 41, *41,* 57
Evans, Richard, 6–7, 99
exterminators, 48–49

Fahnstock State Park, 92
falcons, 33, 75
fawns, 2, 4, 20, *26,* 72, 84, 87
   with deformed legs, 31–32,
     39
   how to help, 113
   injured, rescue of, 64, *65,*
     68–70, *69, 70*
   nursing of, 7, 113
   see also deer
fear:
   defecation and, 47
   survival and, 4, 16

federal government, wildlife
and, 19–20, 96
feeding, 4–11
of baby birds, 9, 11, *12,* 59,
87, 97, 111
of infant animals, 7–11, *10,*
17, *26,* 38
of omnivores, 4
of sick or injured animals, 4,
6, 11
through tube, 7, *8, 9, 10,*
38
first aid for wildlife, 110–114
Fish and Wildlife Service, U.S.,
20
fishermen, marine animals and
birds attacked by, 95
fishhooks, birds injured by, 56,
57, 101, *102,* 112
food chain, DDT in, 75
forestland, decline in, 27
forests, national, 20, 98
foxes, 81
fur coats, 106

game:
wildlings classified as, 20
see also hunting; trapping
game birds, 20, 75
gangrene, 32–33, 35, 36, 111,
113
geese, Canada, 45–46
government, *see* federal
government, wildlife and;
state governments
grouse, 21
gulls:
herring, 11
sea, 82
Guy, Maxine, 96–97, *96*

habitats:
destruction of, 19, 27, 93
population level and, 77
Hardhat (bird), 18
"harvesting," of game animals,
20, 89
hawks, *40,* 75, 93, 99
red-tailed, 23–24
Heath, Beatrice, *102*
Heath, Ralph T., Jr., 101, *102*
Help for Hooked Birds (Heath),
101
Help Our Wildlife (HOWL),
93, 94, *94*
herons:
great blue, 39, 97
green, 4
herring gulls, 11
horses, wild, 107
Humane Society of Marin, 94
hummingbirds, 97
hunting, 25, 75–78, 89, 106,
108
animal defenders and, 98
balance of nature and,
77–78
as contest with animals or
birds, 76–77
of endangered species, 20,
75
game classifications and, 20
"harvesting" and, 20, 89
population regulated by, 77,
107
primitive people and, 76
on public lands, 20, 70–72,
97–98, 107
by raptors, 75–76
species weakened by, 77
state regulation of, 20, 97,
107

interns, *see* student interns
intravenous feeding, 6

Johnson, Debbie, 93

Kamchi, Andrew, 87–89
kangaroos, 4

Lapine, Judy, *8, 10,* 11, 17,
　42–46, *43, 44, 70,* 86
Laura, Jim, 84–85, 87
leghold traps, 35–36, 81
Lerman, Mark, 4, 6, 13,
　31–41, *32, 34, 40, 43,*
　45, *50,* 51, 57, 58, 70,
　72, 81, *92*
　dedication of, 38–39
　in Lifeline's early days, 21,
　　23, 26
　surgery performed by,
　　31–34, *33,* 36
Lewis, Betsy, *8, 9,* 16, 17–30,
　35–36, 38, 39, *40,* 45,
　57, 58, 59, 75, 82, *92*
　injuries of, 23–24
　Lifeline founded by, 17–21
　in Lifeline's early days,
　　21–26
　making rounds at veterinary
　　hospital, 3–4, 6–13
　mission of, 26–30
　as vegetarian, 76
Lifeline for Wildlife, *iv,* 1–92,
　103, 110
　credo of, 4
　early days of, 21–26
　education program of, 42–43
　fund-raising for, 24
　injured wildlife rescued by,
　　54–57, 64–70, *65, 66, 68,*
　　69

Lifeline for Wildlife, *cont'd.*
　mission of, 16, 26–30
　origins of, 17–21
　pet-sitting service of, 24, *28,*
　　43, 82
　records kept by, 33–34, *41,*
　　59
　release procedures at,
　　70–72, *73*
　state officials' relationship
　　with, 24–25
　Stony Point center of, 92, *92*
　student intern program at,
　　24–26, 82–92
　surgery at, 31–34, *34,* 36
　veterinary hospital of, 1–16,
　　92
　volunteers at, 54–60, 85–
　　86
　wild animals relocated by,
　　45–46, 47–51, *51–53*
　see also Ellenville, N.Y.,
　　Lifeline facility at
littering, 109

Maloney, Carol, 54–57
Marine Mammal Center,
　101–103, *103*
marine wildlings, 95, 101–103,
　103
marsupials, 4–6
Monsey, N.Y., Lifeline
　veterinary hospital at,
　1–16
Monterey County SPCA, 94
moose, 20
Morales, Jamie, *iv*
mountain lions, 95
mourning doves, 81
Mouska (woodchuck), 17–18
muskrats, 2

National Educational Television, 106
national forests, 20, 98
National Rifle Association, 98
National Wildlife Federation, 106
National Wildlife Rehabilitators Association, 35, 99
New York, deer hunting in, 20
nighthawks, 93
nocturnal animals, 79–82
nuisance-control permits, 48
nursing:
  of infant animals, 7–11, *10,* 17, 38, 113
  of infant birds, *9,* 11, *12,* 59, 87, 97, 111
  by marsupials, 4–6

omnivores, 4
opossums, 3, 4–7, *5,* 16, 33, 41, 81, 89
  anesthetics for, 34
  habitat of, 6
  as marsupials, 4–6
  orphaned, how to help, 5–6, 113–114
orphaned wildlings, how to help, 5–6, 110–111, 112–114
Osofsky, Steve, 31, *34,* 36, *38*
otters, 95
overpopulation, 77, 107
owls, 33, 72–75, *74,* 82, 93, 99, 101

parasites, 36
parks, state, 20, 98, 107
Payne, Marc, 45–53, *61,* 72, *73, 74, 74,* 78, 79, 82, 84, 92, 101

Payne, Marc, *cont'd.*
  in rescue operations, 64–70, *65, 66, 69, 70*
  training and job experiences of, 46–47
  wild animals relocated by, 45–46, 47–51, *51, 52*
Peking ducks, 54–57
pelicans, 94–95, 101, *102*
permits, for rehabilitators, 20, 97, 110
pesticides, 20, 27, 60, 75, 81
pets, 16
  caught in traps, 36
  Lifeline's boarding service for, 24, *28,* 43, 82
  returned to the wild, 1, 4, 13, 81, 82
  wildlife harmed by, 21, 109
  wildlings as, 1, 42, 90, 96–97, 110
pheasant, 20, 75
pigeons, *9,* 11–13, *40*
pinnipeds, 103
Plesko, Valerie, 2, 7, 11, 57–58
poisons, 95–96, 107
  pesticides, 20, 27, 60, 75, 81
pollution, 19–20, 27, 60
population control, hunting and, 77, 107
primitive man, hunting by, 76
Progressive Animal Welfare Society (PAWS), 93, 94
Project Wild (curriculum guides), 108

quail, 20, 75, 97

rabbits, 4, 18, 30, 54, *55*

rabbits, *cont'd.*
  orphaned, how to help,
    112
rabies, 109
raccoons, *3,* 11, 21, *21–22,*
    34, 36–38, *37, 38, 52,*
    53, 58, 89, 93
  caught in chimneys, 49, *50*
  at Ellenville facility, 13, *14,*
    15, 41, 49, 79, *81*
  infant, how to help, 112
  as nocturnal, 79
  as pets, 1, 4, 13, 90
  released into the wild, 1, 4,
    13, 41, 60, *61–63,* 92
  relocation of, 47–51, *51–53*
racing pigeons, 11–13
ranches:
  so-called, for fur-bearing
    animals, 106
  sheep, 95–96
Ranger Rick (magazine), 106
Raptor Research and
    Rehabilitation Center,
    99–101, *99*
raptors, 33, 74–76
  DDT and, 75
  flight cages for, 95
  rehabilitation centers for, 75,
    99–101, *99, 100*
  slaughter of, *75*
record keeping, 33–34, *41,* 59,
    95
Redig, Patrick, 99, *100*
release into the wild, 16, 41,
    60, *61–63,* 70–72, 84, 87,
    89, 92, 97
  of birds, *iv,* 13, 18, 29, *73,*
    75, 81–82, 86, *90,* 101
  of former pets, 1, 4, 13, 81,
    82

relocation of wildlife, 45–46,
    47–51, *51–53*
rescues, 86
  of injured wildlife, 54–57,
    64–70, *65, 66, 68, 69*
rights of animals, 47, 89, 103,
    105–106
robins, 81

San Francisco SPCA, 94
Schneider, Joe, 47–48, 49
Schwartz, Ria, *61–63,* 70,
    85–86, 87–88, 89
seabirds, 95, 101
sea gulls, 82
sea lions, 101–103
seals, 101–103
sea otters, 95
sheep ranchers, poisons used
    by, 95–96
Sierra Club, 110
Simpson, Cindy, *44*
skunks, 2, 4, 79, 80
  infant, how to help, 112
  rescues of, 86
snapping turtles, 51
songbirds, 93
sparrows, 1–2, 13
SPCA's (Societies for the
    Prevention of Cruelty to
    Animals), 64, 94,
    101–103, 110
  see also ASPCA
squirrels, 1, 3–4, 13, 23, *43,*
    44, 79, 93
  infant, feeding of, 7, *10*
  orphaned, how to help, 112
  returned to the wild, 81
Stahl, Shari, 2, 3, 6, 11, 17,
    58–60
starlings, 18, 21, *73,* 86

state governments, see wildlife
managers
state parks, 20, 98, 107
Stony Point, N.Y., Lifeline
facility at, 92, *92*
student interns, *26, 27, 28, 30,
73,* 82–92, *84*
duties of, 82–85
program initiated for, 24–26
reflections of, 86–90
Suncoast Seabird Sanctuary,
101, 102
surgery, 31–34, *34,* 36, *100*
amputation, 33, 72
anesthetics in, 33–34
for deformities, 31–32, 39
swans, 87–89
Swenson, Paula, *100*

trapping, 25, 106, 108
on public lands, 20, 70,
97–98
state regulation of, 20, 35,
97, 107
traps:
injuries caused by, 35–36
leghold, 35–36, 81
releasing animals or birds
from, 36, 111, 113
Treehouse Wildlife Center,
99
tube-feeding, 7, *8, 9, 10,* 38
turtles, 2
snapping, 51

vaccinations, 48
vegetarianism, 76
veterinary medicine for wildlife,
33

Wallburg, Diane, *61–63*

Washington State Wildlife
Rehabilitation Council, 93
Wenz, Donna, 87
Whisper (owl), 74–75, *74,* 101
George Whittell Wildlife
Rehabilitation Center,
94–95
wildlife management, 20
wildlife managers, 19–20, 42
hunting and trapping
regulated by, 20, 35, 97,
107
Lifeline's relations with,
24–25
permits and licenses issued
by, 48, 97, 107
wildlife protection, funds for,
107
wildlife refuges, 20, 97–98
wildlife rehabilitation, rewards
of, 16, *30,* 78, 86–87, 90
wildlife rehabilitation centers,
93–95, 99–104
how to find, 110
specialized, 99–103, *99,
100, 102, 103*
see also Lifeline for Wildlife
Wildlife Rehabilitation Council,
35
wildlife rehabilitators:
individuals as, 96–97
permits for, 20, 97, 110
professionalism among, 99
wildlife veterinary medicine, 33
wildlings:
domestic animals vs., 42
feeding of, 4–11, *8, 9, 10,
12,* 17, *26,* 38, 59, 87,
97, 111
hazards to, 19–20, 27–30,
75, 93, 95–96, 109

wildlings, *cont'd.*
   how to help, 109–114
   as pets, 1, 42, 90, 96–97,
      110
   relocation of, 45–46, 47–51,
      51–53
   rescues of, 54–57, 64–70,
      65, 66, 68, 69, 86
   returned to the wild, iv, 1, 4,
      13, 16, 18, 29, 41, 60,
      61–63, 70–72, *73,* 75,
      81–82, 84, 86, 87, *89,*

wildlings:
   returned to the wild, *cont'd*.
      90, 92, 97, 101
   surgery on, 31–34, *34,* 36,
      39, 72, *100*
   *see also specific species and
      topics*
Wisconsin Humane Society, 94
woodchucks, 17–18, 64–68,
      66, 68, 70, *89*
woodpeckers, 93
worms (parasites), 36

About the Author

Patricia Curtis has written many books and magazine articles about animals. Of *All Wild Creatures Welcome,* her eighth book, she says: "I've tried to tell a true story which makes the point that the wild creatures we share the earth with are not ours to exploit. In my opinion, wildlife rehabilitation encourages compassionate thought and action in people, and is a civilizing force that's ultimately good for all of us."

Ms. Curtis is the mother of two adult children and lives in New York City with her dog and four cats.

About the Photographer

David Cupp is a writer-photographer whose articles and pictures appear frequently in *National Geographic Magazine.* He and Patricia Curtis also collaborated on *The Animal Shelter* and *Cindy, A Hearing Ear Dog.* He lives with his wife and four children in Denver, Colorado.